PR

"Sara Hosey's wit and wisdom bring to mind Ali Smith and Lucia Berlin. Her stories resonate with love and sympathy for the women and girls of the poor, working, and middle-class navigating life under an oppressive, simpering patriarchy. Her characters are smart, funny, bold and wonderfully flawed. Sara takes us all over the dirty underside of the suburbs of Wisconsin and New York, but really—spiritually—of every small town and outskirt in America. This is a book I will keep coming back to."

JOEL MOWDY, AUTHOR, *FLOYD HARBOR*

"Absolutely stunning! Sara Hosey's *Dirty Suburbia* contains some of the most poignant, insightful, and entertaining stories I have read in ages. I couldn't put this book down. Perceptive, empathetic, and always on point, Hosey's characters will stay with you. I was awestruck by the range of tales and will be thinking about the world of *Dirty Suburbia* for a long time. These stories are absolute gems. Not to be missed."

KELLY FORDON, AUTHOR, *I HAVE THE ANSWER*

"Gritty and darkly funny and ultimately humane."

JESS WALTER

ABOUT THE AUTHOR

Sara Hosey is the author of three young adult novels: *Iphigenia Murphy, Imagining Elsewhere,* and *Summer People.* Her short fiction has been shortlisted for the Katherine Anne Porter Prize and the American Short Fiction Halifax Ranch Prize and has appeared in journals like *Cordella Literary Magazine* and *East by Northeast Literary.* She is a parent, a community college professor, and a tree enthusiast.

sarahosey.com

DIRTY
SUBURBIA

SARA HOSEY

www.vineleavespress.com

Dirty Suburbia
Copyright © 2024 Sara Hosey

All rights reserved.
Print Edition
ISBN: 978-3-98832-040-7
Published by Vine Leaves Press 2024

No parts of this publication may be reproduced, stored in a retrieval system, or transmitted in any form or by any means, electronic, mechanical, photocopying, recording, or otherwise, without the prior written permission of the copyright owner.

This book is sold subject to the condition that it shall not, by way of trade or otherwise, be lent, resold, hired out, or otherwise circulated without the publisher's prior consent in any form of binding or cover other than that in which it is published and without a similar condition including this condition being imposed on the subsequent purchaser. Under no circumstances may any part of this book be photocopied for resale.

This is a work of fiction. Any similarity between the characters and situations within its pages and places or persons, living or dead, is unintentional and coincidental.

Cover design by Jessica Bell
Interior design by Amie McCracken

For Jess, John, and Julian

CONTENTS

Christine
11

Dirty Suburbia
35

Land Mammals
63

Blessed Virgin
91

Not for Everyone
121

Revenge of the Nerds
159

Elephant Realty
185

Another Eden
207

Back to the Beach
233

Mickey Makes a Salad
261

Acknowledgements
287

CHRISTINE

Gina and Stacey, twelve and almost-thirteen, ignore the little kids. Gina and Stacey are busy, sweating in the full sun, sitting on the swings in the playground of their former elementary school, talking about *General Hospital* and about Marie, a girl from junior high with whom they are obsessed.

But then one day Christine comes through the fence to the swing area. The little girl isn't paying attention and walks right in front of Stacey's swing. Stacey has to break and swerve, send her legs to the side as the chains loop crazily. Stacey looks around for an adult to scowl at, but there is none.

The little girl has perched herself on the adjacent swing.

"Push me?"

***

That first day, at the swings, they are confounded by about Christine's aloneness.

"What's your name?" Stacey asks.

"Christine."

"Where is your mom? Is she here?" Gina asks.

"No," the girl answers. "Nana will come back for me later."

The big girls touch the tips of their sneakers to the black rubber matting beneath them, their swings floating in figure eights. Christine's feet dangle, nowhere near the ground.

"We'll take care of you," Stacey concludes.

***

And they do, throwing themselves into the project of Christine with the enthusiasm of adolescent girls during an unstructured summer vacation. They buy her ice creams from the truck, teach her how to play handball and, one day when Stacey remembers to bring a comb, untangle Christine's hair and put it in a fishtail braid.

They bring their Barbies to the park and, shielded by Christine's presence, act out elaborate romantic plots. They push her on the swings or let her sit on their laps while they talk about Marie's breasts or critique *General Hospital*—it is only this summer that they have begun to notice repetitions and inconsistencies, only weeks now since they have begun to sometimes cynically laugh at their beloved show.

They boss Christine around and chide her and pretend her requests to be carried exhaust them, that they are long-suffering, put-upon, but devoted, little mommies.

***

An ancient woman, silent and stooped, deposits Christine at the park each day, appearing again in the afternoon to fetch her. The old woman doesn't speak English.

They ask, "But where are you from?" and Christine shrugs, says, "Rego Park," with her unfamiliar accent.

"But before that? Where is your family from? Your nana?"

Again, the shrug. Christine looks away.

"Like, I'm Italian," Gina tells her. "And Stacey is Jewish."

"Italian and Jewish," Stacey corrects her.

"Maybe she's Spanish?" Gina says.

Stacey shakes her head. "She's not Spanish."

"Do you speak Spanish?" Gina persists, lowering her face to Christine's.

"Ice cream?" Christine asks.

***

In addition to not being Spanish, the woman is not Christine's grandmother; she is Christine's great-grandmother. This fails to register as important to Stacey and Gina, however, for whom advanced ages—those beyond twenty-five or thirty—are too obscure to hold meaning.

Their understanding of younger ages, however, is highly articulated. Stacey believes that the gap in Stacey and Gina's ages—five months—explains any discord that arises between them. Stacey, for example, has great disdain for Gina's sloppiness, her carelessness. She is like a little kid, forever rushing and spilling and dripping and staining. Although, Stacey knows, this is really because Gina's mother is also sloppy and careless.

Gina and her mother live in a dirty apartment from which, Stacey knows, Gina is evicted each morning, told not to return until dinnertime. Depressed second cousins and drunk uncles crowd the apartment. "We can't go to my house," Gina might tell Stacey. "My mother's ex-sister-in-law is crashing on the couch and she needs to sleep all day." She might add, "she did my nails," and flash violently red fingertips that will only last a few hours before Gina will start gnawing, peeling the polish off with her teeth, and spitting it onto the pavement.

Stacey's house, in contrast, is too-empty. Her stepfather and mother and older brother flee each morning, one after the other, and when Stacey emerges from her bedroom, the stillness of the house can become loud like the ocean in a seashell, unbearably loud, and Stacey has to stop herself from screaming, from running out the door. And so she goes to the park, arriving before Gina to sit on a bench and eat a Pop-Tart or a powdered donut and pretend to read a paperback.

In the mornings, it is mostly little kids and their mothers who stand unsmiling and smoking as their children play in the sandbox, a square of yellow dirt littered with candy wrappers and, Stacey knows because she has seen, cat pee. By the time Gina arrives, the Korean boys—eighth graders and their older brothers—have come to play handball. In the afternoon, it is mostly white boys playing basketball and the first shift of an endless parade of multicultural groups of terrifying teenagers, who slouch and swear on the perimeter benches, the girls like explosive devices, detonating at irregular intervals, leaping up to slap someone or to toss a lit cigarette in a boy's face.

***

Stacey and Gina are both summer-brown overlaid with pink sunburn on their shoulders and cheeks. They press their forearms together to compare the white watch-shaped swaths of skin on their wrists; they talk daily about the development of their tans, about "laying out" in preparation for wearing bikinis to the beach, which they will never do; or will do one broiling Saturday, a harried parent loading them into a station wagon, but only that one time in the whole hot summer.

Little Christine's skin is pale though, so pale you can see the blue veins on the soft insides of her arms. It makes Stacey want to pinch her.

***

Stacey and Gina agree that Christine's abandonment at the park is startling and offensive, further evidence of Christine's family's difference.

Gina and Stacey have only been allowed to come to the park by themselves since last summer, when Gina was eleven and Stacey was turning twelve and, although they never told their mothers, even that was too early.

The harassment was stunningly immediate, as though Stacey and Gina had tripped an invisible alarm that alerted all area perverts to the presence of parentless pre-teens. Their very first day in the park, a man had hailed them from the street, called them over to his car, ostensibly to ask directions. Polite girls, they approached to find that in his fist he held his penis: peach-and-red mottled meat. Stacey gasped, pulled her friend's arm, and they dashed back to the park.

Another day, sitting on the swings, they became aware of a man staring, openly and aggressively. The girls fled and he followed them with a chilling, practiced casualness. They were smart, though, and led him to a neighbor's house before cutting through the backyard and shutting themselves up in Stacey's garage, which was where her stepfather had his workshop. They strung fishing line across the door as a boobytrap and armed themselves with a staple gun and a hammer. They shouted, "Come and get us!" to the roof beams, hoping he would stumble in, and they could murder him or at least hurt him, humiliate him. "Queens Girls Nab Perv," the *Daily News* headline would read. And beneath it, a color picture of Stacey and Gina standing beside their trophy, strung up like Jaws.

Now they are older and, of course, the harassment continues. Men still say vile things, expose themselves. But the girls have gotten better at seeing it coming, moving out of the way, averting their eyes, pretending not to notice.

***

"She probably thinks we're free babysitting," Stacey says, as the great-grandmother recedes one morning.

"She's lucky we're here," Gina says. She has brought scissors to cut the little girl's bangs so that her hair won't always be in her eyes.

***

One day, Christine does not appear.

Gina chomps on grape gum, spitting out each piece as soon as it loses its flavor and sticking a new one in her mouth. Stacey finds the grape smell heavenly, tempting, but she has braces and must decline each offered piece.

"Maybe she's sick," Stacey says.

"I hope she's okay," Gina says.

They miss their little girl. The day is long and hot and shapeless, the afternoon stretching out before them like the uncrossable expanses of sand in the movies they watch, with *General Hospital* at 3:00 an impossibly distant oasis.

The swings are flat metal benches attached to chains. Gina and Stacey stand and swing themselves so high that the chains hiccup and buckle, and their bodies fly free for a moment before they are yanked bank, their long hair rushing forward and sticking to their faces. Sometimes Stacey believes she will continue right over the top and around again, and she wonders if she will survive.

***

Christine is back the next day, unable to account for her absence.

"But what did you do?" Stacey asks. Christine sits between them on a curb next to the concrete water fountain. The day is ugly and thickly hot.

Christine gazes past Stacey, her beautiful black irises set on ivory eyeballs. "TV." She adds, "Buy me ice cream?"

"I don't have any money today," Stacey lies. She feels exploited because Gina never has any money and never brings any snacks except for gum, which she knows Stacey can't have.

Stacey can't imagine Christine's existence beyond the park. They ask her questions all the time, but the girl's answers are vague, almost cagey:

"Do you live in a house or an apartment?"

"Yes."

"Does your grandmother live with you too?"

"Nana takes care of me."

Over her head, they roll their eyes at each other.

Christine rips a round scab from her knee and raises it to her mouth. Gina pushes her hand away. "No," she says. "That's gross," even though, Stacey knows, Gina eats her own scabs like it's her job.

Gina turns to Stacey. "I wonder what happened to her yesterday." She touches the ends of Christine's hair and wrinkles her nose.

"They obviously don't care about her," Stacey says. It makes her so angry to think about these people, Christine's family, people she can't quite imagine, who think it's okay for a little girl to be in a park alone. It makes her angry at Christine, too, for not being fearful, for trotting around the park, happy and unafraid, confident that others will take care of her, protect her.

"They don't deserve her," Gina agrees. Christine sets her chubby finger on the curb, in the path of an ant, who bumps into it before turning and heading the other way.

"We should bring her to my house and give her a bath," Stacey says.

The moment Stacey says it out loud, she is shocked to realize that the longing to bring Christine to her house has always been there, invisible and waiting, like an adult tooth. And now it is pushing through, erupting, inevitable.

She expects Gina to demure, but the other girl agrees.

"Yeah," Gina says. She puts her face in front of Christine's face. "Would you like to go to Stacey's house? We could watch TV and eat animal crackers." She turns back to Stacey. "Do you have any animal crackers at your house?"

***

It's so easy.

"What's wrong?" Stacey asks, pretending nonchalance. They are already walking toward the front gate.

"Don't leave me," Christine says, trailing behind them.

Stacey stops walking. She puts her arms around the girl and picks her up. "Don't cry," she says.

"It's okay," Gina adds, rubbing the girl's back. "We just want to go to Stacey's. You can come with us."

"Nana said I don't leave the park without her," Christine murmurs adorably.

Gina and Stacey nod. This is good advice, of course, although it clearly doesn't apply to them, to this situation. Christine belongs to them. They take care of her every day. They will simply take care of her somewhere else.

"Stacey lives just around the corner. We could bring you back before your nana comes and she won't know you ever left."

The girl wipes her nose on the back of her hand.

"Animal crackers," Stacey sing-songs, rocking the girl.

"Okay," Christine says at last. "But you will carry me?"

***

At first it is thrilling to be inside the cool and empty house. They sit on the big couch in the small TV room, dusty blinds pulled against the day, eating animal crackers out of a clear plastic barrel, and watching *The Price is Right*.

"We could play school," Gina says. "Do you still have that chalkboard upstairs?"

Stacey shrugs; she doesn't want to play school. She likes being here in the den together, but she is also beginning to wonder if this was a mistake. She looks at Christine and Gina and knows that her mother wouldn't like this, a little girl she doesn't know in their house eating their animal crackers. Stacey hears a dog barking outside and feels annoyed that they never go to Gina's, that it will be her who gets in trouble if anyone finds out about this. She knows it was her idea, but somehow it feels like Gina's fault.

"What if her grandma comes looking for her?" Stacey says.

"She never comes before 2:00."

"But what if she does."

Gina takes a handful of animal crackers. "I don't know." She eats them and then sticks her finger deep into the back of her mouth to dislodge where the cookies stick behind her teeth. The sight of it makes Stacey want to puke. "She'll probably think we took her for a walk or something."

"She might call the police," Stacey says.

"No," Gina says. She puts the fingers she just had in her mouth into the plastic jug of cookies. Stacey looks at the TV to avoid seeing. "Do you think she would?"

"She might."

"She doesn't even speak English. How could she call the police?"

"Don't eat all the animal crackers," Stacey snaps. She hears the soft rumble as Gina takes another handful anyway. "She could ask someone else to call."

"She won't do that," Gina says. To Christine she says, "You're having fun, right? Isn't Stacey's house nice?"

Stacey looks and the girl nods and smiles, her own teeth plastered with chewed cookie.

***

When Christine goes to the bathroom, they wait outside the door.

"Should we give her a bath now?" Gina asks. Stacey considers it. The girl's head, when she was carrying her, smelled rich and salty.

"Her grandmother might be angry if we bring her back and she's too-clean. She might suspect something."

Gina nods, deferring to Stacey's wisdom.

"I guess we should get going soon anyway," Gina says.

When the girl comes out of the bathroom, though, they say nothing else about leaving. Instead, they make orange juice from a frozen can, the noise of the wooden spoon hitting the sides of the plastic jug like a heartbeat, like home. They smile and let her lick the spoon. They pour tall glasses and put ice cubes in them.

It is 2:00 and then 2:30.

They watch *General Hospital*. Stacey has dug out an old Rainbow Brite coloring book and a handful of crayon stubs, and Christine sits on the floor, coloring on the coffee table. Stacey is nervous and distracted, but in the game she is playing in her head, she is calm because in the daydream Christine lives here too, even if they have to hide her in the evenings. There are many precedents for this in the sitcoms Stacey watches, stories about children who care for exotic, mysterious creatures like sea monsters or aliens or lifelike robots. Stacey knows better of course; she can't keep Christine. But she wants to pretend a little longer.

"It's so late," Gina observes. She peels paint off of her finger nail with her teeth and then plucks the paint from her tongue and wipes it on her shorts. "What are we gonna do? Could we just walk her back and then run away?"

"The grandmother might see us," Stacey returns, as though that settles it, although she is not feeling settled at all.

"We could bring her back and then run away as fast as we can. The grandma would never be able to catch up with us."

"But she'd be able to identify us," Stacey says. Her eyes dart to the clock on the VCR. Her mother will be home at 5:30.

Gina groans but then stretches out on the sofa, digging her cold little toes under Stacey's thigh. Stacey pushes her feet away. "So what are we gonna do?"

Returning to the park seems impossible, as though in coming to Stacey's dark house during the day, they have stepped outside of time. The park feels far away or gone somehow, like Stacey's grandmother's house after it was sold and torn down, a brick Fedders building rising in its place.

"We haven't done anything wrong," Stacey says. "We're taking care of her," she reminds Gina, a deliberate note of impatience in her voice. Then, to Christine she says, "Do you want to have a sleepover?" The girl looks back without comprehension.

"What?" Gina asks, confused. She scootches her body up on the couch.

"If I said I was going to sleep at your house and you said you were going to sleep at my house," Stacey begins, talking over Christine's head. "We could stay in the garage. I have sleeping bags."

Gina scrunches her nose but then relaxes. She smiles and shrugs, warming to the idea. Stacey's heart beats hard.

***

Stacey's stomach is sour and her skin prickled. She is afraid her mother will sniff out the deceit and will say no, you may not go to Gina's, and then what will she do?

In the kitchen, she hovers near her mother. She is tempted to tell her the truth, to blurt it out and get it over with. She is a big white pimple, ready to pop with the slightest pressure. She will be in so much trouble. Will her mother call the police?

"Can I stay at Gina's tonight?" she asks, her mother pulling boxes from a high cabinet.

Her mother's eyes twitch and almost settle on Stacey, but then they move on. She takes the wooden spoon from the counter and uses it to dislodge a box of Hamburger Helper that she can't quite reach. It is fine with her if Stacey goes to Gina's. Will she be eating dinner there?

Stacey takes her knapsack—the garage has already been stocked with sleeping bags and stuffed animals, apples and a jar of peanut butter, Barbies, a tea set, and the chalkboard—and lets herself out the side door. She walks down the block and then cuts back through the neighbor's yard and returns to the garage.

Arrived at last, she sees that Christine is crying. Gina explains that the books they brought out—*Harriet the Spy* and *Bridge to Terabithia*—are too old for the little girl. She doesn't like them.

"Well, play Barbies or something," Stacey snaps at Gina, crouching beside Christine. "Or we can play school?" she says more gently, to Christine. But they have forgotten to bring the chalk, Gina tells her.

"Don't cry," they say, gently patting the little girl. "We'll take care of you."

***

It is something new, Christine cowering away from them. Stacey wants to apologize, to reassure Christine, but there is something else happening within her as well. She doesn't mind, entirely, the girl being afraid.

Stacey scolds, "I said, enough. You are safe with us. I said, stop crying or I will give you something to cry about." She knows she is using her mother's threats, threats that have made Stacey herself cry harder and Christine, predictably, sobs. "She is driving me crazy," Stacey says to Gina. "She is driving me up a wall."

Just as Stacey once caressed and carried the child, this is a kind of playing too, and Stacey, not gently, takes Christine from Gina's lap and holds her in her own. She squeezes the girl's arms too tight in a bear hug, but then Christine leans into her, and Stacey's anger is instantly replaced with tenderness. She should not have snapped at Christine. The little girl is scared. Stacey lets go of Christine's arms and presses Christine's head against her shoulder and says, "Shush."

"Maybe we should bring her back to the park," Gina says.

"What?" Stacey cries. "It's the middle of the night!"

"No," Gina says, looking at the clock over Stacey's stepfather's workbench. "It's only 9. If we left her at the park now, no one would see us. I bet her grandmother would just find her in the morning."

Stacey shakes her head. "You are so dumb sometimes. We can't leave her in a park by herself at night."

"We could call 9-1-1 and tell them she's there."

Stacey rocks the girl in her lap. "She's fine. You're fine," she says. Christine relaxes. She puts her arms around Stacey's neck and Stacey thinks that it was all worth it, before she registers warmth on her leg and she pushes Christine away, sliding the girl off her lap and onto the ground, to the cool concrete. "What is wrong with you?" Stacey hisses.

"What happened?"

"She peed her pants. And she got it on me too. What is wrong with you?" she says again. "Why didn't you just tell me you had to go?"

The girl is truly crying now, her head back and her mouth open in a half-moon.

"Be quiet," Stacey demands. Whatever it was she was trying to do is slipping farther away from her, just as the girl does, as she rises from the floor and moves toward the door, howling. Stacey is up and in two quick steps has a hold of the girl's arm. She spins her around, slaps her across the face.

Everyone is surprised, except perhaps Stacey, who suddenly knows that the slap was there, waiting in her palm, all these weeks since that very first day Christine found them in the park.

Christine is silent and stunned for a moment and then inhales, preparing to cry anew. Stacey pulls the small, stiff body toward her again. "I'm so sorry," Stacey says. "I didn't mean to do that. I just wanted you to be quiet."

"It's okay," Gina says, although it's not clear who she is talking to. "Everybody calm down." She touches Stacey's arm. "Let me change her. We have extra clothes."

Stacey releases Christine, allows Gina to take the girl's hand and wipe her face with a paper towel. Christine whimpers, her breath coming in hiccupping gasps. Gina peels off the girl's shorts and underpants. Stacey and Gina pretend not to look at Christine's private parts as she steps into the too-big shorts. Stacey retreats to the corner to change her own clothes.

As if answering a question, Christine says, "I want to go home."

"Don't you like it here, with us?" Gina asks, her voice too-sweet and quavering. She looks at Stacey over the girl's shoulder, her eyes big and scared.

Stacey thinks of the police; she imagines them rolling slowly down her block, looking for signs of the little girl. Will Christine say that Stacey hit her?

She wishes, more than anything, that Gina hadn't been there, hadn't seen that. She hates that she hit the girl. She hates that Gina saw her hitting the girl.

"I want to go home," Christine says again.

"We'll take you home," Stacey says. "Tomorrow." She approaches carefully and does her best to appear patient and pleasant. "We're having a sleepover!" Christine looks at her blankly. Stacey places her palm on the girl's hot cheek, the same spot where she struck her. "It's an adventure?" she tries. She withdraws her hand and adds, raising her eyebrows with mock-impatience, as though she is forced to explain the simplest, more reasonable thing: "We're taking care of you tonight and you'll be back home tomorrow."

Although her breath remains uneven, Christine doesn't cry. She watches Stacey steadily, warily.

Stacey doesn't look away. She says to Gina, "We should probably turn out the lights. Go to sleep."

"I guess," Gina says, sitting on her sleeping bag. She arranges the oversized Care Bear under her head and reclines. "Christine, want to sleep next to me?"

Christine nods and finally looks away as she moves toward Gina.

Stacey, her jaw clenched and her heart beating in her temples, tries to act unbothered as she unfurls her own sleeping bag on the floor beside them.

The garage is orderly and clean, concentric rings of tools and hulking machines with lines like early jet planes, at the center of which they've set up their camp.

She turns out the light but leaves the lantern on low and gets in her sleeping bag. The floor is hard, but it smells nice, like sawdust and oil and the earth.

***

"We'll really have to give her a bath now," Gina says, the girl between them. "And can we do laundry in your house tomorrow? Or should we go to Goodwill and try to buy her new clothes?"

Stacey doesn't answer. She listens to the second hand of the wall clock, like the chug-chug of a gentle train.

"We are bringing her back tomorrow, right? We can't keep her any longer," Gina says.

Stacey is disgusted. How had she not realized before how stupid Gina was?

Gina was right about one thing though: they should have dropped Christine back at the park earlier. At 2:00 or at 4:00 or even at 10:00. With every minute that passes reasonable explanations recede; return feels more impossible.

Stacey hears a distant voice, hears pounding music from a car stereo. She cannot figure out how to bring Christine back to the park. She thinks—only for a moment—but she does think it—that maybe they will have to kill the girl and bury her in the backyard. That there is no other way to undo this.

***

Christine sleeps but wakes often, crying. She tries to rise, but Gina pulls her back, tells her it will be all right, it's almost time to go home.

In the morning, Stacey, empty and alert, watches out the small window. Her mother and stepfather and brother finally leave. Stacey takes the pee bucket and tries not to look at the dirty yellow as she dumps it next to the garage. There is not much in there, but the smell is loud and makes her head hurt. "Come on," she hisses, and Gina and Christine hurry in the backdoor to use the bathroom properly.

Gina wants cereal, Gina wants to give the girl a bath, Gina wants to change clothes, but Stacey says no, no, no. There is no time. "We have to get her back to the park," Stacey says. She is decisive now. "The earlier the better. We'll bring her close to the park and then leave her and she will have to find the rest of the way herself."

Christine is tired and not-crying, but she is not happy either. She is mewling and talking to herself in another language. She pulls on their hands and says she wants to go home.

"Yes," Stacey tells her. "You are going to go back to the park. But you have to go by yourself. We are going to take you close to the school and then you have to go the rest of the way. Do you think you can do that?"

Christine doesn't answer.

"You're going to have to," Stacey says. She has given Christine animal crackers in a Ziploc baggie, as though the girl is Hansel and Gretel and they are the evil stepmother. Or maybe they are the witch, sending the child back home again, thinking, it was all a misunderstanding, it was just a mistake. Stacey isn't clear; maybe a fairy tale analog doesn't exist for their situation. "You have to look both ways and then cross the street and then you'll be at the school. You know that the playground is right behind the school. And if your grandma is not there, if Nana is not there, you sit on the swings and wait."

Gina leans close to Stacey's ear. Her breath is hot and smells of Lucky Charms. "What if someone tries to kidnap her?"

Stacey thinks she will cry, then, in front of them, but she doesn't. Instead, she starts to laugh, so hard, too hard, and Christine looks at her, confused. Gina smiles a little and giggles, as though she had meant to say something funny all along.

***

Christine walks between them, holding their hands. They have tucked the Ziploc baggie into her shorts.

Stacey is watching all around, looking out for police cars or nosy neighbors as they walk down her block and then onto the avenue. The girl's hand is sticky. She is wearing the dirty clothes again—now stiff and smelly.

Halfway down the block, they pry her hot hands from their own. Stacey, breathing in shallow gasps, tells Christine, "You have to go by yourself now. Straight and then cross the avenue. Look both ways. And then you'll see the school."

Christine is crying. "No, no, no," she begs. She grabs at their hands again, but she can't get purchase; they wriggle away. "Don't leave me." But Stacey and Gina look at each other over her head. Gina nods and then they run, as fast as they can, the opposite direction of the school. Before they turn the corner, they look back. The girl is still standing there, watching them.

There is no shade on this hot dry day and the sidewalk shimmers, as though diamonds are embedded in the concrete.

"Come on," Stacey says. "We don't want her to follow us."

***

They tell their mothers they are sick, and their mothers think they've just had a falling out, that's how girls their age are, inseparable one moment and then angry, roiling with resentment the next. They stay in their rooms, in their beds, although Gina calls Stacey one day and they make a plan to go to the park that evening to make sure she isn't still there, a week later, wandering the handball courts or waiting at the swings.

They meet on the avenue, the air swampy and the sky still bright. Not talking, they creep toward the park. What do they expect? The police to spring a trap? Christine's nana waiting to scream at them in a language they don't understand? A crawling, reaching, child-skeleton, like the kind in cartoons about the desert?

But the playground is empty, except for the teenagers, drinking beers on the monkey bars.

DIRTY SUBURBIA

Sue took off her headset and signaled to the manager that she was going on break. The "big heist"—she was the only one who called it that, and she didn't think the others were aware that she was being sardonic—was scheduled to take place that night.

She used the payphone to call Matt. Her whole body pulsing, as though in her anxiety she had transformed into a huge, beating heart, she lied and told him she couldn't drive what the others were definitely un-sardonically calling the "getaway car."

"I just talked to Christopher," she told Matt, a slight squeak in her voice. "I have to go up north. It's my mom. It's time."

"Babe," Matt said. "That sucks."

"Yeah," she agreed. "I'm so sorry I can't be there. Can you call Kiera? Do you think she can handle driving the car?"

"You don't have to worry about that."

"But will you call her?" Sue asked.

"Yeah, yeah—I'll call Kiera now."

"Good. It's gonna be awesome." Sue forced herself to smile. An authentic fraudulence: Sue knew herself well enough to know that she would have pretended enthusiasm even if her mother's impending death was the reason she had to miss the "big heist." "It's probably better to have Kiera drive anyway," Sue continued, her voice quivering, although, again, not for the reasons she'd led Matt to believe. "My nerves are shot."

Matt was quiet for a moment and Sue did hope, in that pause, that he would say, *Fuck it, I'll come up north with you to support you at your dying mother's bedside.*

But he didn't. Instead, he said, "Yeah, you might be right."

***

Matt had first proposed the idea for robbing the video store he worked at (the "big heist"), a few nights earlier. He'd emerged from the Premiere Video with DVDs tucked under his arm, coat unzipped despite the Wisconsin-winter cold, and ducked into the car, tossing the stack of movies to the floor.

"Get anything good?" Sue had asked as he leaned across and kissed her cheek. She snaked the car through the empty parking lot, taking the long way, past the only place still open, the China Café.

"Not really. Cal and Kiera asked me to pick up *There's Something About Mary*."

"I wanted to see that one too. What else?"

"A bunch of crap. *Pulp Fiction* again. *Back to the Beach?* And *Pink Flamingos* again." Matt dug out his cigarettes, lighting one before rolling down the window just a crack, the cold air slicing into the car.

"You didn't get the Pam Anderson sex tape?"

"I did not."

Sue sucked her lips in protest.

"You can come in and rent it yourself," he said.

"You're not embarrassed to serially watch *Pink Flamingos* but you won't watch the Pam Anderson sex tape with me?"

"I didn't say I wouldn't watch it. I'm just not renting it." Matt scooted up in his seat. "I don't want everyone I work with knowing … whatever." Sue wondered what whatever was, and why it mattered. "And *Pink Flamingos* is like art, or something," he added. "Anyway, I told Cal and Kiera we'd swing by tonight. Drop off the movie. Hang out."

Sue only blinked a little harder than normal before humming her assent, adding, "I'm gonna come into the store tomorrow and rent that fucking sex tape."

"I was thinking," Matt said, ignoring her and looking at himself in the darkened car window. "We should rob the video store. I've been thinking about it all day."

"Whatever. I don't mind renting it," Sue said. "I'm not as easily embarrassed as you are."

"No, I mean, like, go in with a gun and rob the cash register."

"What?" Stopped at a red light, Sue had looked at her handsome boyfriend. He didn't look back at her. She collected herself and said, pretending to smile placidly, "Go on."

***

Cal, Matt's manager at Premiere Video, lived alone in an apartment on the far east side of Madison. That's where they all lived, Cal and Matt and Sue: out past the Bucky Badger flags on the college kids' squat houses, out past the Tibetan prayer flags on the east side hippies' ramshackle Victorians. Cal and Matt and Sue lived way all the way out in dirty suburbia, in the land of mostly-derelict strip malls and off-brand Olive Gardens called things like "Primavera!" They lived in ugly, low-slung apartment buildings that accepted Section 8 vouchers, their exteriors a ghastly white with mismatched, dangerous-looking prosthetics: hastily-added ramps for the senior citizens, rusted awnings, rickety fire escapes.

Not Kiera, though, Cal's girlfriend, a graduate student originally from New York. No, Kiera lived with roommates in one of those peeling-paint Victorians near the Willy St. Co-op. How she had met Cal was a mystery, but that a grad student from New York was dating the manager of a Premiere Video who lived out in dirty suburbia told Sue everything she needed to know about Kiera, which was this: she wasn't as smart as she thought she was.

She wasn't that smart and she wasn't that cool. She apparently had a good marijuana connection, but, Sue thought, not even clouds of pot smoke disguised the scent of misfit that hung around Kiera, like a haze, a low-hanging fog.

Nevertheless, Sue and Matt's interactions with Kiera and Cal had recently intensified, becoming an almost-daily thing, approaching a casual familiarity, like siblings on a couch, unselfconscious of their closeness.

Sue, who had learned, had really learned, to pick her battles, was letting it go, at least for now. People liked Matt—women in particular loved Matt—because he was good-looking and macho but seemed unthreatening, sort of helpless and gentle. Those were the things that Sue loved about Matt too. She also loved that he needed her, desperately, even if he didn't always realize it. Matt could barely function in the world without her, honestly, which was a lesson he learned the few times they'd broken up and he'd come back, once literally on his knees.

***

"What's up," Matt called as he and Sue let themselves into Cal's apartment that night, the night he'd proposed robbing the store, the same night that Sue had started to see what was really happening, the picture emerging like one of those magic paint coloring books, the colors popping no matter how recklessly you swiped your watery brush.

The apartment was too-hot and filled with smoke and terrible music.

"What is this shit you're listening to?" Matt asked, stomping the snow from his boots.

Sue left her coat on the floor and sat next to Kiera on the couch. Kiera, with wide, watchful eyes, scooted over.

"Dave Matthews is awesome," Cal answered, unfurling himself from the papasan chair and heading toward the kitchen.

"Why are we friends with people who have such bad taste in music?" Matt asked Sue as he crouched to investigate the piles of CDs on the floor next to the boom box.

"If we suck so much, why'd you come over?" Cal called from the other room.

"We're here to smoke our fucking faces off," Sue said, picking up the pipe on the table. This was performative—she never got too high—but she raised her eyebrows and flashed a brief, insincere smile at Kiera before lighting the pipe and inhaling once, shallowly, all the while keeping the other girl in her peripheral vision.

Matt popped a CD out of its case and apologized to Sue: "Eminem. It's the best thing he has."

"You don't like Eminem?" Kiera asked.

"My brother's gay," Sue said, looking at Kiera as though she was the absolute stupidest person on the planet. "So ..."

This was not strictly true, as Sue's brother hadn't officially come out (although everyone had known since the beginning of time that Christopher was gay). And Christopher himself loved Eminem, gleefully rapping along about killing "fags."

No, Sue's distaste for Eminem had other origins. A fellow white Midwesterner of a certain class, Eminem was familiar to her. She felt as if he was someone she'd gone to high school with who was now suddenly famous. And she felt as though he might recognize her, too, that with his flat, shark eyes, Eminem would take one look at Sue and see her for exactly what she was: a fucking jellyfish, blindly floating along, stingers stretching toward any soft flesh careless enough to get close.

Soft flesh like Kiera's. Kiera was always just there, too dumb to get out of the way.

***

Matt had risen from the CD player and walked toward Sue, a sexy cowboy-saunter, his eyes locked on hers. Sue would have preferred to have gone "out" instead of sitting around Cal's disgusting apartment. She would have liked to have gone to one of the bars, in large part because she loved the way other people looked at Matt. She liked to watch people watching him and to feel them watching the both of them, Matt and Sue, the two best-looking people in most rooms. As he made his way across the bar to give her a kiss and sit beside her, everyone would know that Sue wasn't just pretty. She was something special. The most handsome guy in the bar was in love with her.

But even stuck at Cal's, Sue smiled at him as she lit her American Spirit. Matt smiled back. And then she saw in the dim light that his eyes flitted over to Kiera.

Sue didn't turn. She didn't need to. She knew what Kiera looked like. Kiera was round-faced and soft-bodied and she wore strange, stupid clothes that she found in thrift stores. Her shit-brown eyes were enormous, bovine, sexy-cartoonish, but also a little vague, perhaps one of them a little lazy. Sue didn't need to turn to see Kiera sitting there, watching everyone with her big, crazy, fuck-me eyes.

Instead, Sue said, "Have you guys watched the Pam Anderson sex tape yet?"

"Shit," Cal said. "I didn't know hot girls liked porn."

"It's not porn," Sue said, rolling her eyes but enjoying a little spike of pleasure at his remark.

"Uh, yeah it is," Kiera said.

"Oh my god," Sue snapped at Kiera. "It's not a big deal."

"No one said it was a big deal," Kiera returned.

"Sue's obsessed," Matt said, sitting on the floor in front of the coffee table.

"I just want to see celebrities naked," Sue said. "I mean, doesn't everybody?"

"I don't," Kiera said. "I think the whole thing is exploitative."

"Give me a fucking break," Sue said hotly, and Matt, uncharacteristically tuned-in, reached between the bottles and ashtrays on the coffee table to rest his hand on Sue's forearm.

"Babe," he said gently. He squeezed and then took his hand away. "She's under a lot of stress," he explained to the others.

"What's up?" Cal asked, adjusting his wire-rimmed glasses.

When Sue, continuing to gaze through the curling cigarette smoke, didn't answer, Matt said, "Her mom's real sick. Cancer."

"That sucks," Cal groaned. "What kind?"

Sue gazed at him, studiously blank-faced. "Breast."

"My aunt had breast cancer," Kiera said, nodding sympathetically. "Really bad. She—"

Sue cut her off. "I don't give a shit about your *ant*," she said, repulsed by that New York accent. "And don't even try to tell me that she died. You don't tell someone whose mother is probably gonna die of breast cancer that your aunt died."

Kiera's silence told Sue that the dumb cunt's aunt probably had died.

"Sorry," Kiera said at last, her mouth turned down at the corners. "I'm really sorry, Sue." Sue watched Kiera look to Matt. "But the treatments are so good these days."

***

There'd been only one girl before—a hippie named Nan—who'd ever been a true cause for concern. Matt had been bartending at the time, and though the job itself was short-lived, the Nan-thing persisted, like a winter cold that carried over too far into the spring, and it started to make Sue nervous.

Sue was particularly offended by Nan's appearance—her corduroy and clogs, her unsexy piercings—all of which made Sue wonder what would happen if she let her own platinum hair go the brown of dirty snow, if she started wearing comfortable underwear and flannel shirts. Is that, she wondered, what Matt really liked?

In the end, clearly, it was not. And Sue hadn't had to lift a finger. She didn't ask for the details, but she'd had to bail Matt out—he said for "fighting," but the charge was domestic violence—and immediately after that, Nan put a restraining order on him.

Sue was magnanimous, agreeing that the bitch was obviously a psycho, vindicative, that Nan was, ultimately, the problem.

Sue didn't have to point out that she'd never called the cops on Matt or put a restraining order on him, although, as they both knew, she certainly could have.

***

"Me and Sue were talking on our way over here," Matt said that night at Cal's, still sitting cross-legged at the low table. "We have an idea."

Sue took a long pull on her beer. "The big heist," she said.

"What's going on?" Cal asked, leaning forward in his papasan, intrigued.

"It's not a fucking threesome," Sue tried to joke. "Or foursome," she added, waving vaguely in Kiera's direction, pretending to pretend to be polite.

"We're robbing the video store," Matt said.

Cal leaned back, disappointed and skeptical. "What are you talking about?"

"What's in the register on a typical night?" Matt blew out his lips, shaking his head, blown away by the obviousness of it all. "It would be so easy. Sue drops me off right before closing, when you're working. I wear a mask and wave around my pop pop's rifle. Unloaded, of course. You give me the money and lay down on the floor. I head out the back door to where Sue's in the getaway car. You wait ten minutes before calling the cops."

Cal sat forward again. "You could conceivably get more if you took some DVDs too," he said. "The new ones. To sell."

"Dude, that's so smart. See, Sue. I knew Cal would be cool." Matt leaned forward now, too, as though it was only him and Cal talking, as though Sue and Kiera were groupies.

"Wait, you're not serious?" Kiera interjected. She looked to Sue, incredulous, seeking an ally. Sue shrugged, smiling like she was the Mona Fucking Lisa. Sue wanted to be on whatever side Kiera was not.

"But why?" Kiera said turning back to Matt and Cal. "And what ... why are you even involving Cal?"

"Well, I'm not a real robber," Matt said, smiling indulgently. "Plus, I didn't want to scare the shit out of him."

"I totally would have recognized your voice, man," Cal said.

"But ..." Kiera remained aghast. "I mean ... why? Do you need the money that badly?"

Matt had looked down into his beer bottle, as though he were embarrassed, and then he looked up and Sue saw it again: just a flicker of his eyes. But in that flicker, Sue saw an appeal to Kiera, a reference to something shared.

Sue rose and went to the kitchen, her fingers tingling with rage. She took a beer from the refrigerator and closed the door, but then opened it again and took out another and held them both in one hand, the bottles clinking in between her fingers. She was so thoughtful. She'd bring Kiera a beer too.

Returning, she heard Kiera say, "You don't need to do this."

Matt cajoled: "Aww, come on. You and Suzie can drive the getaway car."

Sue placed the bottles on the coffee table and sat. She noticed that Kiera's first beer was still full.

"Are you not drinking?" Sue heard herself ask, the question coming out nastier than she'd intended. "Are you pregnant?"

Kiera turned her head and looked at Sue through narrowed, canny eyes. Sue, her lips parted, a nasty laugh waiting to escape, didn't look away. Then, with a jerk, Kiera rose, bumping the coffee table and knocking over one of the full beers. She hesitated, but didn't stop to right it, before scurrying out of the room.

Sue watched the liquid dribble out of the upset bottle.

"What the fuck was that?" Cal asked. When Sue looked at him, he flapped a hand in the air. "Just leave it. I'll clean it up later."

Matt, his face pinched, picked up the half-empty beer and took it with him, going to stand next to the darkened window. "I don't know why you always have to be such a fucking bitch to everyone," he muttered. Sue followed his gaze. Outside, the falling snow, which looked pretty in the cone of yellow light from the streetlamps, was slowly covering over the old snow, soaked-gray piles that ringed the parking lot.

It's still there, though, Sue felt like saying. *The old snow is still there, underneath, you know.*

"Don't worry about Kiera," Cal said, as though they were still talking about the video store. "She seems like a square, but she's a fucking nut."

***

Sue put it together later that night, lying in bed beside the gently snoring Matt, the truth making itself plain like the threads of the conversations she facilitated at the Relay Center. At the center, she sat in a cubicle and typed messages to the hard-of-hearing and then, in turn, read aloud their messages to hearing friends, an elaborate system in which Sue was trained to act as the medium, to remain neutral as to the messages. And while much of her job was boring, Sue made a game of guessing the subtexts, of trying to discern the shape of the stories by how their words glanced off the truth, revealing that which was left unsaid.

She imagined moderating a relay call between Kiera and Matt: Kiera saying that she was pregnant and Matt, stupid Matt, telling Kiera how happy that made him.

And then Kiera, asking if Matt was really prepared to be a father, go ahead. ("Go ahead"—that's what you said when you were done speaking). And Matt typing back yes, he had never been more ready, he was really going to turn things around, and they would start a new and beautiful life together, but that he couldn't leave Sue, not right away, because Sue's mother was dying. Go ahead.

Sue wanted to interject (which at work was a fireable offense). She wanted to say, I am here too, I am listening, and what he is saying is not true, it is not accurate. He can't leave me because he can't hold down a job and because I pay the rent and all the bills and I own the car and I drive him around because he hasn't had a license in years. But more than that: he can't leave me because we are forged together, we are MattandSue. Before we had each other we were like orphans in this world and yes, mistakes have been made, but we belong, in the end, to each other, and this belonging although sometimes shameful, is also undeniable. You may not go ahead.

It didn't matter that Kiera was pregnant. That bitch could get an abortion. She'd better get a fucking abortion. Sue would fucking see to it.

***

After she'd let Matt know she couldn't drive the getaway car, work was brutal: she still had two hours left, and there weren't any good calls—arguments or the delivery of bad news—to distract her. Finally, she got one of the calls that the less-seasoned operators found upsetting: perverts or giddy teens who typed filth so that she would have to speak it aloud to their accomplice: "I love you I want to suck your cock I have big tits. Go ahead." She'd been instructed to disconnect immediately on those calls, but Sue let this one go on, counting down the minutes until the end of her shift, reading in a deadpan, thinking, *what else you got?*

When her shift was finally over, she went to the Crystal Corner, a place that she and Matt didn't usually go. The front windows of the bar were made up of smoky glass blocks, like huge, dirty ice cubes, and Sue sat on her stool, looking at those ice cubes, chain smoking and nursing a beer. Over the classic rock from the jukebox and the satisfying smacks of balls colliding on the pool table, she talked to a toothless old man who said he was a Vietnam vet.

"My dad was in Vietnam too," Sue told him.

"Oh yeah?" The man, whose name was Keith, squinted at her. "What'd he tell you about it?"

Sue shrugged. "Nothing. He didn't like to talk about it."

"Hmm," Keith said. "Was he a good father?"

"No," Sue told him. "He fucked off for good when I was nine." She lit a cigarette. "Before that, he did seasonal work in the Dells."

Sue saw the words she spoke aloud in illuminated blue letters, as though typed on a screen, and she laughed.

Seasonal work in the Dells. That told you all you needed to know about her dad.

"I used to spend a lot of time up in the Dells too," Keith said, his face creased with concentration. "There was one particular strip club up there I used to frequent. Maybe I knew your father."

Sue shrugged. "Maybe." She looked Keith in his watery eyes.

"It's like that, then," Keith said. "Well. His loss. A pretty daughter like you. But still. Family's family. Dads are important. Want some oxy?" He held out a handful of blue pills.

"Thanks," Sue said. "I'll take some for the road." She plucked two pills from his dirty palm and put them in her jeans pocket.

There was a time before her father had left, when things got especially ugly, and Christopher, two years younger than Sue and already her near-constant companion, began to physically crowd her, crawling into her bed at night, sitting too close at the breakfast table, finding her on the blacktop at school. He'd hold her hand or put a finger through the belt loop on her jeans or tickle her ear or place his foot over her foot, like a playful dog. Once, when he leaned into her, his shoulder pressed against her upper arm, Sue shrugged away, bellowing, "Stop! Why are you always touching me?"

Christopher said nothing in the moment, but later, lying next to her in bed that night, he'd whispered, "If I'm not touching you, I'm afraid I'll die."

Sue told him he wouldn't die, reminded him that he was in school all day without her. But when he fell asleep and his hand fell away from her arm, she put her own hand on his back and left it there all night.

She missed her brother, who still lived up north with their mom, and she resolved to call him more, be a better sister. Maybe he could come down to Madison, stay with them for a while. He might enroll in classes at MATC, as she had, one optimistic autumn before things had gotten difficult again with Matt, and she'd been too embarrassed to return.

She looked at the clock over the bar. "Dads are overrated," she told Keith as she slipped from her stool.

She used the payphone by the bathroom to call the police. "I overheard some people talking about a robbery—a big heist—over at the Premiere Video on the east side," she told the dispatcher. "They'll be getting there in a few minutes. The getaway car will be out back."

She left the bar and headed home. She figured that if Matt made it back to the apartment, she'd tell him a miracle had occurred: her mother had recovered and Sue hadn't had to go up north after all. The oxycodone was a stroke of luck, and would serve as a happy distraction from her lie.

And if Matt didn't come home, she'd take an oxy herself and go to sleep. In the morning, she'd wait for a phone call about bail.

She wouldn't bail Kiera out, or Cal, if it came to that. She knew Kiera had parents, back in New York, and Sue imagined they would swoop in with their money and their lawyers; maybe they'd even usher her back east somehow.

But the cops would hold Kiera, Sue thought, at least for a little while. Ideally, they'd convince her to turn on Matt. Sue smiled, thinking about how uncomfortable things were about to get for Kiera, thinking about how she was introducing Kiera to a whole new, inconvenient, and expensive world of involvement with the criminal justice system.

***

When someone pounded on the apartment door, Sue actually leapt up from the ancient couch, heart beating so hard that she was afraid that something inside her would pop and burst. She stabbed out her cigarette and then stood very still, blinking, hoping whoever it was—whoever had slipped in through the building's broken front door—would go away.

But the thumping continued, and was followed by a muffled voice: "I know you're in there."

Sue walked quietly across the room and opened the door.

Kiera made a face to suggest that Sue was the biggest idiot she'd ever met, and barreled in, kicking off her snow boots, talking before Sue had a chance to close the door behind her. "I thought you were with your mom," Kiera said, indicating with an eye roll that she'd hadn't thought this at all. She took off her coat and handed it to Sue.

"I'm leaving in a little—why? What happened at the video store?"

"Why don't you tell me, Sue?" Kiera said, pursing her lips.

"Did you drop Matt off?"

Kiera nodded.

"And then what happened?"

"I drove away."

"But you were supposed to wait out back," Sue began. "Did you chicken out? He's gonna..."

"I suppose he'll get arrested," Kiera interrupted. She flung herself on the couch. "Or else he won't, and he'll walk back here and be super-pissed. But I don't think he'll be showing up here because I think you did us dirty."

Sue turned her back to Kiera and slung the coat over an armchair. She felt Kiera watching her. She wished they were having this conversation over relay, that she could have time to collect herself before responding. But she wasn't, and she didn't, and so she asked, "Why would I do something like that," hating herself for the tremble in her voice.

Kiera didn't answer and Sue, her back to Kiera, squeezed all the muscles in her face and then relaxed them, so that she would appear blank, calm, unconcerned. Then she turned around. Kiera, scowling, waited. She should simply say it, Sue thought. There was nothing she was too embarrassed to say.

"You need to get an abortion." Sue sat in the chair in a way that she hoped conveyed that the matter was, in fact, settled. And then, she couldn't help herself. "Go ahead," she added.

"I'm not going to do that," Kiera said.

Sue cleared her throat. She considered saying it again, just telling the other girl what needed to happen. Instead, she said, "Matt belongs to me. He's my boyfriend. My fiancé."

Kiera snorted. "Fiancé," she said. "Where's the ring? Did you guys set a date?"

Sue ignored her, looking at a spot on the wall just above Kiera's staticky hair. "You're making a mistake. Believe me. I've seen this before. You're not important to him."

"That's not what he says."

The living room was small and cramped and the only thing between Sue and Kiera was a trunk that served as a coffee table. Sue looked at the trunk and then picked up a pack of cigarettes, even though she didn't really want to smoke, and pulled one out, lit it.

"You're in over your head," Sue said at last, her voice high and limned with a whine. "You don't really know him. You've never seen him mad."

"I've seen him mad," Kiera said. Although she couldn't look at her directly, Sue observed that Kiera had sunk down into the couch—"sitting on her neck," Sue's mother might have said—and Sue wondered why she had even come over.

"Not really," Sue said. "He can get violent."

"He's never been violent with me," Kiera said, flatly. "I wouldn't stay with him if he hit me." She scootched up a little, her attention caught, at last, just a tug on the fishing line, but a move that made Sue feel there was something—someone—on the other end. "What are you saying? Are you saying that he hits you?"

Sue let out a small, dry laugh. An image flashed before her: the sink filled with old food; he hadn't bothered to scrape his plate into the garbage, and she'd had to use her fingers to pick macaronis and ground beef out of the drain. She shouldn't have said anything, but she did, and then the next thing she knew he'd smashed a glass on the floor and then his palm was against her cheek, her face pressed against the wall. She tried to speak, and she sounded adorable, her lips forced into a pursed position, "Please," she'd said, and it came out, "pwease."

But that was a while ago now. That was in the fall. And it hadn't even been that bad, though they did have a discussion afterward. Promises had been made. And things had been better, sort of. Although now there was this.

Sue looked at Kiera.

"Why would you stay with him if he hit you?"

"Because." Sue cast her eyes around the room, as though the answer was just on the tip of her tongue, as though it was so obvious, she couldn't find the words. "Because." She wished she'd taken those pills earlier; she wished she'd been emotionally checked-out of this conversation. Because she didn't think she would be able to say out loud that Matt was the only good thing in her whole fucking life. Because. Because she hadn't had the money or time or intelligence to finish community fucking college, and because she didn't want to work at the Relay Center for the rest of her life, and because her mother was useless, and her brother was a loser, and because the best part of her week was walking into the Palace Bar and Grill with her hot fucking boyfriend, his arm around her shoulder, her fingers clutching his belt. She felt her throat tightening, her eyes getting hot. "Because we love each other."

"That's bullshit."

"What do you know? You don't know anything about it. You have everything," Sue cried out. "You already have everything." She imagined how she might look to Kiera and her mind skittered, searching for purchase, for a way to take back the conversation, to push down and away the hot shame that Sue felt creeping up, through her fingers, into her chest and throat and face.

"I don't even know what you're talking about," Kiera said.

"You're in grad school. You're rich. You have parents."

Kiera laughed again, but it was a mean, incredulous laugh. "I hate my parents. I don't even speak to them. You're not the only one on the planet who—" Kiera began.

Before she could finish, Sue said, "Matt is mine."

"Yeah, but he's not," Kiera returned.

Sue took a deep breath and knew, suddenly, that she would cry in front of this strange, confusing person; later, she knew she would be ashamed to have cried. Or maybe she wouldn't. It didn't matter because in that moment it was irresistible. Sue felt as though she been throwing herself against something solid and unmovable. Kiera, it seemed, had, without much effort, worn her down. The tears slid into the sides of Sue's lips.

"Why do you even want to stay with him?" Kiera asked, apparently unmoved by the tears. "He cheats on you. And you just told me he, like, physically abuses you." Kiera leaned forward, her big eyes wide and looking, Sue felt, straight into her. "And you just set him up and had him arrested."

Sue hiccupped and inhaled unevenly. "I mean, it doesn't sound so great when you put it that way," she said, trying for sarcasm, but tilting her head to one side, hinting at the hit. She put a hand over her eyes and rubbed, hard.

Kiera got up and left the room. She came back with a roll of toilet paper and handed it to Sue.

"I can't believe you," Sue said finally. "You're going to have a fucking baby with him?"

Kiera nodded.

"What about Cal?"

"Cal?" Kiera said. "He's a zero." She shrugged and sat back down. "A placeholder."

"But Matt... he just robbed a video store. You want to have a baby with a felon?"

"Honestly, I don't know," Kiera conceded. "But I think I'm in love with him. I'm kind of … curious to see what happens."

Sue snorted. "Curious. What is wrong with you? You can go ahead and bail him out, then, if you're so curious." She shredded the cheap toilet paper in her hand.

"We'll see about that," Kiera said, almost cheerfully. She leaned again toward Sue, her brown hair falling forward, over her shoulders. "You'll be okay," Kiera said, almost impatiently. She squinted. "You'll probably be better off without him. Try to muster up some dignity. This is your chance to get out, once and for all." She shook her head, as though it was all so obvious. "You're so beautiful. You'll meet someone who treats you the way you deserve to be treated. Maybe this is your chance to really make a change."

Sue grunted, incredulous.

"I'm doing you a favor," Kiera continued. "If you want, I can even tell him what you did, that you set us up. If you need him to break up with you—"

"You're a fucking psycho," Sue said. "I didn't realize that until right this minute. I thought you were a nerd, but really you're a psycho."

Kiera laughed. "God, why are you so mean? I don't know why you hate me so much."

"You stole my boyfriend!"

Kiera shrugged and smiled grimly. "I guess … when you put it like that it doesn't sound so great."

Sue left her cigarette smoking in the ashtray and stood. She began to pace the small room, shaking out her hands, flexing her fingers.

It hurt; it hurt more and in a different way than any of the many other times she and Matt had broken up. If those had been toothaches, this was the empty hole left behind: tender meat, vulnerable, frightening. She felt like it might kill her.

She thought of Matt in the mornings, his softly sour breath, his sweet and stubbly face pressed into the pillow, pulling her into the bed next to him, waking up smiling and telling her he loved her.

"So, your mom though," Kiera said. "Is she okay?"

"My mom's fine," Sue said, blinking hard. She stopped pacing and faced Kiera. "She did have cancer. That was true. But she's been in remission for months."

"Wait," Kiera said, an open-mouthed smile spreading across her face. "Who's the fucking psycho?"

Sue looked out the window. It was snowing again. There was no sign of Matt. She imagined him in the back of a police cruiser, the red and blue lights reflected on the falling snow, and a manager from the China Café stepping out to see what the commotion was. She imagined Matt in the holding cell, leaning into the pay phone, wiping his nose on the sleeve of his hoodie, maybe crying a little. When he said, "I need to make a collect call," would the operator hear the desperation in his voice, his regret and shame and need? And then, when Sue didn't answer, would he call Kiera next?

She looked back to see Kiera watching her, smiling a little, maybe enjoying it all a little too much. "Fuck," Sue said.

"Do you want me to leave?" Kiera asked, making no move to get up.

"No," Sue said. She crouched beside the stack of DVDs next to the television and, with shaking hands, picked one up. "Wanna watch a movie? I have the Pam Anderson sex tape." She cast a glance over her shoulder. "Or is it too exploitative?"

Kiera chuckled. "I'll watch your porno with you," she said.

Sue loaded the disc and turned the lights off before she took her place on the couch.

"Don't tell him I set him up," Sue said.

"Okay. But you better not try to frame me. You better not tell him it was me who called the cops," Kiera said severely.

Sue made a noise: she was impressed, unbelieving. Her mind, so accustomed to such strategizing, had automatically explored that path, like water from a dammed stream, seeking survival, and she hadn't entirely abandoned the idea. "How did you know?" she asked. "I won't, but I might have."

Kiera laughed. "Maybe you're not as mysterious to me as you are to other people."

Sue couldn't stop herself. "We're not going to be, like, friends after this," she said.

"I know," Kiera said. "But we can be friends tonight. Now be quiet. I'm trying to watch this dirty movie." Kiera shifted and stretched her legs out along the couch, resting her ankles on Sue's thighs. "Is this okay?" she asked.

Kiera's legs were warm and heavy.

"It's fine," Sue said. She took each of Kiera's feet, the toes like bird bones inside the fuzzy socks, and held them gently in her hands. The movie was immediately bright and lurid, Pam's voice filling the room. Sue began to cry again, just a little. Kiera didn't seem to mind. Still, Sue was grateful for the blue-black dark.

LAND MAMMALS

After a lecture and lunch, a minibus transports the Americanists to Walden Pond. A small, kind, divorced man named Caleb sits beside Lexi. They talk about their colleges, their dysfunctional departments (Lexi not disclosing that she, like the Wanderer of Old English poetry, is newly adrift, unmoored), and then finally, pathetically, their cats and cat-sitting arrangements as the town gives way to suburb and farmland and then ancient oaks and unmanicured brambles and then again to order, to a parking lot and a visitor center.

Disembarking the minibus, Caleb lingers, waiting for Lexi, but she pretends to check something on her phone, trailing off to the side where he cannot reasonably follow.

Dor, the group leader, a sickly-looking older woman who probably believes that old lie about how it is impossible to be too thin, launches into a well-rehearsed lecture about native plants, and Lexi looks up and around at the sprawling, intricate canopy. As the group follows Dor away from the parking lot and further into cool woods, the asphalt and gasoline and bus fumes fade, replaced with smell of dirt, air heavy with rain, and green leaves, fully alive.

The trail arrives at a small cabin, a recreation of Thoreau's original. Thoreau himself sits in the doorway, whittling. Lexi shivers, suddenly aware of the sweat pooling in her lower back.

That morning, she had woken to wonder about the ghosts that supposedly haunted her room at the Concord Inn. The man at reception, stooped and older, his skin the same yellowish tint as the fading wallpaper, making Lexi wonder if he was chameleon-like, somehow unconsciously camouflaging himself, had widened his eyes as he'd delivered her key the previous day. "Number 204 is haunted," he'd informed her. "That's what they say, at least. Do you mind?"

"I love ghosts," Lexi had told him, unsmiling. But she had taken two Xanax before bed, so even if there were ghosts, even if they'd swirled around her, whispered in her ears, slammed the closet door, or tickled her feet, she wouldn't have roused.

And there had been no evidence of ghosts in the morning. In fact, she'd felt so profoundly alone—even though she could hear the murmurs of other guests in adjacent rooms, water rushing through pipes, the slam and click of a closing door across the hall—that, as she dressed for breakfast, she wondered if she was simply too boring, that the ghosts had wandered into other, more exciting rooms.

"You should come back tonight," she'd announced to the ghosts who probably weren't even listening. "You won't want to miss it. I'm having a threesome with Emerson and Fuller. I'm bringing home Henry David Fucking Thoreau."

She'd been kidding, of course. And yet now here he was: Thoreau, whittling in front of his house.

***

"Good morning," Thoreau says, looking up from under his straw hat, putting his tools gently on the ground, and standing. He wears a white shirt tucked into brown trousers, suspenders, brown boots. He has an unkempt brown beard that crawls down his neck. His skin matches his shirt; the entire palette just a handful of the same shades. He has the wild eyebrows of an older man, but a youthful, almost-boyish face. A very convincing Thoreau, Lexi thinks. "Welcome to my solitary dwelling," he says. He gestures toward the open door and walks through it.

Thoreau takes off his hat as the group arranges themselves in the cool room, holding their bodies carefully in this small space, trying not to touch any objects or each other's hot, sweaty skin. Lexi, crammed into a corner, finds her view of Thoreau obscured.

"You'll pardon me, I've only three chairs," he begins. "Although I have a great deal of company in my house, especially in the morning, when nobody calls." There is an amused murmur from the group; they wait for him to continue. "But I am no more lonely than the loon in the pond that laughs so loud, or than Walden Pond itself. I am no more lonely than a dandelion in a pasture, or a bean leaf, or sorrel, or a horse-fly, or a bumble bee."

Dor is nodding, practically vibrating with delight.

"I keep very busy," Thoreau continues. He talks about his beans and about his furniture and the bread he bakes.

Lexi listens, aware that she is inexplicably attracted to him, to this Thoreau, perhaps because of this morning's declaration, but perhaps not. She tries for a moment, to puzzle it out: is it the man playing Thoreau or Thoreau himself or simply the idea of Thoreau? She has never had a thing for Thoreau before; she would have thought Emerson more her type. Or maybe Nathaniel Hawthorne, who was actually kind of a hottie when he was young. She realizes, dimly, however, that it might simply be that this Thoreau is the man talking, the man that they are listening to.

And are they ever listening. Scanning the room, Lexi sees faces ranging from adoring to self-consciously indulgent to skeptical. Dor is rapt, smiling like a parent at a school play. Caleb tilts his head and narrows his eyes, and Lexi imagines that he is waiting for a misstep, hoping to catch an error, to show-up this Thoreau. These are her colleagues, these neurotic, ill-dressed people, academics who, like Lexi, were selected to participate in a program of intensive study in historic Concord, Massachusetts. "Nerd camp," she'd explained to her sister Shannon when they'd made the arrangements for their mother.

"Oh," Shannon had said, and through the phone, Lexi could hear her purse her lips in distaste. "I didn't realize they had that sort of thing for adults."

"I mean, I'm looking forward to it," Lexi had clarified.

"You would," Shannon had said.

Perhaps Lexi would have enjoyed the experience more, however, if she hadn't felt quite so much like an adolescent on vacation with bird-watching aunts and uncles, a sneering teen treated alternately with good-natured forbearance and outright contempt. Or perhaps it is that this trip has brought into focus just how frightened she is by the life she feels cementing around her, a life of books, yes, which was what she has always said she's wanted, but also apparently a life of loneliness, a life lived on a semester schedule, a life of endless, exhausting, and ultimately unsatisfying, competitions.

It didn't help that Lexi was informed, just days before her trip, that her "line" at the unremarkable four-year college where she taught had "not been renewed," which was a fancy way of saying she'd been canned. It didn't help that, writing-wise, she was drowning in the quicksand-center of her dissertation: she was a PhD, ABD. All but Dissertation: an acronym that disrupted the expected, logical order of letters, leading her to wonder about the missing C. Had its line also not been renewed?

The week should have been a gift, a nice entry on her CV, an opportunity to study. In fact, when she'd gotten her acceptance letter for the program, she'd actually thought that her department chair would be impressed; she'd thought, "This is prestigious. They wouldn't possibly fire me after this!" But then they did: the very next day she got the email full of almost-apologies and an assurance that she could teach as an adjunct, which felt like the equivalent of someone running over your dog with their car and then offering, as a consolation, to let you clean out their hamster cage.

A go-getter, Lexi knew, would use this Concord trip as an opportunity to network, to hustle and self-promote, to find herself a new job. But Lexi had discovered that she was not, in fact, a go-getter. She was more of a let-goer.

And so she hovered at the group's edges, always looking for an excuse for solitude, an exit strategy from group activities. That morning, at breakfast, when Dor announced that they should wear their bathing suits under their clothes for the trip to Walden Pond, Lexi had taken this as her cue to slip away, excuse herself to go change, bringing her coffee and danish back to her still un-haunted room to wait out the minutes until the minibus's scheduled departure.

She'd used the time to call her sister.

Shannon had answered the phone by saying, "I don't know how you do it, Lex." By "it," Shannon meant live with their mother, which is what Lexi had been doing for the past two years. "It's been two days and already I'm going nuts. Honestly. Is matricide even a thing anymore?"

"I'm not sure it was ever 'a thing,'" Lexi had responded. She'd sighed. "Evenings can be tough. If she gets agitated and won't take a Xanax, I usually give her a couple of CBD gummies. She likes them; she thinks they're candy." Lexi looked guiltily at her own contraband stash of Xanax and Valium, pilfered from her mother's supply.

Their mother was only seventy-five, but increasingly demented, which yes, Lexi had learned, really is a medical term for someone who has dementia. Lexi had learned several things about memory loss in recent years, including that this part, this muddy middle, would not be the worst part; that it would seem idyllic compared to the coming days of institutions and paperwork, of confused agitation and outlandish demands, and then patting liver-spotted hands on the arms of wheelchairs, kissing impossibly soft, unresponsive cheeks.

The knowledge that there was something identifiably wrong with her mom, however, was in some ways better than those first strange, confused months, those months during which the mess in her mother's home infuriated Lexi because she did not yet understand that the disorder in her home reflected the disorder in her mother's mind, or rather, perhaps because she did understand it, on some obscure, unexplored level.

Lexi was grateful for the days, or sometimes just mornings, when her mother herself would emerge, when, even if confused, she was often still good-natured, giggling with delight: "Is it really my birthday?

Oh, Lex, honey, I don't even know what year it is!" And Lexi would have been more grateful, but for the days that were increasingly cut through with cruelty, irrationality, vitriol; her mother's sudden mood change like a tooth hitting metal, like the attack of the lap dog, even worse for its predictability.

She'd moved in with her mother, into her childhood home, and they'd hired an aide to come in during the days while Lexi was at school. Lexi told Shannon that she didn't mind moving in with their mom. Lexi's erstwhile job wasn't too far away, and Lexi had no other commitments, obligations, no people attached to her, only a cat named Peanut and many boxes of books. She didn't mind it at all, she told Shannon. She loved their mom. She loved their old house.

Shannon, always so mean, had recently started to insinuate that Lexi had been waiting for an excuse to move back in, that Lexi was incapable of living alone or of finding anyone else who could stand to live with her, that Lexi was a freeloader who had always hoarded their mother, demanded all of her attention, depended on her too heavily. And perhaps some of what Shannon said was true. But still, Shannon didn't want to do it. Shannon hadn't offered to take their mother to live at her house.

And so Lexi and Mom had carried on, mostly happily. In the evenings they watched TV and read; on the weekends, they shopped and, once a month, went to visit Shannon, who lived an hour away.

"There's just been a lot of complaining," Shannon told Lexi on the phone that morning. "Like, a lot. Nothing is the way she likes it. She's very... uncontent. Discontent? Whatever. She's unhappy to be here."

"It's probably confusing for her," Lexi said. "She's probably feeling uprooted."

"Yeah. Well," Shannon said, and it occurred to Lexi that if her sister was a literary text, she would have finished her dissertation years ago, that Lexi could have spun a whole chapter from those two words, the "yeah" curt and slightly incredulous, the "well" likely delivered with raised eyebrows. *The seemingly simplistic, even quotidian response,* Lexi could have written, *in fact gestures to a long and complex history, including Shannon's perception of her younger sister's sentimentality as fraudulent, her belief that her sister was exploiting their mother, and her insistence that her sister was in a state of "denial" about "reality." That is, whether Lexi liked it or not, their mother would be institutionalized—and soon.*

"She wants to talk to you," Shannon had said, and then her mother was on the phone, asking Lexi how the trip was and then in the next breath asking where Ernie was. Frantically, urgently: "I just saw him a minute ago and now I can't find him. He probably needs to go out. Has anyone taken Ernie out?"

"Yes," Lexi assured her, from hundreds of miles north. "Yes, Ernie's been walked." And this was not a lie; the dog had always been walked regularly, fifteen years ago, back when he was still alive.

***

The Americanists ask Thoreau questions: what is he reading? How often does Emerson visit? They reference the Thoreau family history, quote him to himself, and speak dismissively of recent pop culture representations.

Lexi asks, abruptly, "Are there ghosts? Have you seen any ghosts here?"

Thoreau looks at her for a long minute, considering, and she imagines him flipping through the index cards in his head. He lands on a canned answer:

"Just this morning, as the sun arose, I saw the pond throwing off its nightly clothing of mist, and here and there, by degrees, its soft ripples on its smooth reflecting surface was revealed, while the mists," he lifts his hands and wiggles his fingers. "Like ghosts—were stealthily withdrawing in every direction into the woods, as at the breaking up of some nocturnal conventicle."

Dor coos and then offers a small clap, tapping her fingertips together. This is their signal to depart. The Americanists nod their heads, murmur thanks, and file out. But Lexi hangs back, waiting.

This Thoreau, she thinks, is not ugly (as the real Henry David Thoreau undeniably was), but he is not too handsome either. He is just right, as humans go.

After several semesters of teaching affluent young adults, Lexi has recently realized that there aren't all that many truly attractive people in this world. While most people have a few good features—including, for many, youth itself—most have a few bad ones too, and it's the bad ones, the terrible hair or strangely shaped torsos or missing chins, that don't necessarily make them ugly, but force an early forfeit in the big beauty pageant of life.

Lexi herself has never been beautiful. Like most people, she looks fine. She has a decent body and a pleasing overall symmetry, but she is aware that something about her face disqualifies her from being considered "hot" or gorgeous; it is probably her nose-chin combination, which is admittedly a bit witchish.

That Lexi is not a great beauty has always been made perfectly clear by comparison to her fantastic-looking sister. Though Shannon and Lexi share a basic genetic cocktail—their mother had used Kevin, the same sperm donor, for both of them—Shannon's good looks are almost an affront to Lexi, as though Lexi, not Shannon, had been the first pancake.

Their mother had vigorously resisted the old trap of categorizing them, would never brook any nonsense about one girl getting the brains while the other got the beauty. But the world—and the sisters themselves—was not always so tolerant of nuance.

"You could try—a little," Lexi recalls Shannon telling her, as though standing up straight or wearing a certain kind of tennis shoe would transform Lexi, make her suddenly, measurably, more beautiful.

"So could you," Lexi had shot back. "No one ever died of reading a book."

Today, Lexi is wearing a Louisa May Alcott shirt that she had purchased at the Orchard House Museum. The shirt is purple, unsupple polyester, sweetly toxic-smelling. It is incredibly, irresistibly dorky; a tee-shirt she would only wear in the company of other hard-core, unironic nerds.

Suddenly self-conscious, she folds her arms over her chest, but then remembers that the man she wants to talk to is dressed as Henry David Thoreau, and lets them hang again at her sides.

"So, do you like doing this?" she asks. She leans down to look out one of his little windows. There is her group, picking their way through the woods down to the pond.

Thoreau inhales and pauses. He says, "I've very much enjoyed my time here. I came, as I remarked, to live deliberately, to see if I could not learn what life had to teach, and not, when I came to die, discover that I had not lived. Living is so dear."

Lexi shakes her head; she doesn't want to talk to one of the robots in the Hall of Presidents. "Dost thou ever breaketh character?" she asks.

"Ah, Elizabethan English," Thoreau says, a half-smile on his face. "Many of my visitors seem to believe I am much older than I am. Although usually," he adds. "I get the 'thees' and 'thous' from middle schoolers."

Lexi smiles; there he is.

Lexi lets her eyes move slowly over his chair, his little table, his cot. She has always been the person who turns on the faucets in Home Depot showrooms, who longs to crawl into the short beds at the Metropolitan Museum of Art. She's never, however, felt the urge quite as strongly as she does in Thoreau's cabin, this recreation of Thoreau's cabin. Being in a small, carefully curated house has activated a part of her that she has not felt fully since childhood. It is a sense of being transported, of being in a treehouse or a tent, or even in front of a plastic children's kitchen, and allowing the place to act as a portal into your own mind, to be there and to be elsewhere at once. There are no other words for it, no words beyond "play pretend" or "imagine," or at least no words that Lexi knows. It is what she wants to do now; it is what she wants to do with this Thoreau. And yet she also wants to break the spell, to have him accompany her here, in the land of the living, to step outside his story so that they can consider it together.

"How do you get a job like this?" she asks, inching toward the bed.

He looks at her blankly. "As I explained, I came to the woods live deliberately..."

"Yeah, yeah," she interrupts. "But really." She stares openly at the bed. The blanket is wool and brown, like Thoreau's pants. "Have you ever actually stayed here overnight?" Lexi tries.

He says, in a voice of long-suffering restraint, as though she is at last wearing him down, "I sleep here every night, though I did spend one not-unpleasant evening in jail recently."

"Hmm," she says. Although she is too warm in her polyester shirt and her bathing suit has begun to cut into her backside, she is nevertheless at ease here, with this strange man who keeps retreating to his script. And so she does it: she takes her phone out of her back pocket and sits on the bed. She kicks off her flip flops and lays on her side, her head on the single, flat pillow.

Thoreau watches her, alarmed.

"I'm staying at the Concord Inn," she tells him. "They say there are ghosts in my room, but I haven't seen any."

"You probably shouldn't do that," he begins, looking at the doorway guiltily and then back down at her.

Lexi closes her eyes. "Sorry," she says. The wool blanket has a thick, clean smell and the cotton pillowcase is cool on her face. "It was just so inviting." She rests for a delicious moment before asking, "Is this starting to feel like 'Three Bears'-scenario to you?"

"More like a 'call security'-scenario, actually," he says. When she opens her eyes, his brow is furrowed, but he is also smiling.

"Sorry," she says again. She sits up, wiggles her toes back into her sandals. Thoreau watches her. Her phone makes a beeping noise; she has hit a button and Siri asks how she can help. Lexi silences the phone. "My mom used to believe that ghosts communicate with us through our devices," she tells Thoreau. "They use whatever technology is available. That's why they do things like turn lights on and off. And when you get a weird Google result or you butt-dial someone, that's a supernatural interference."

"The Internet as Ouija Board," Thoreau says.

"Yeah. Exactly," she says. She sits forward a little bit. "Exactly."

"Although I'm not sure what you mean by 'Google,'" Thoreau says. "Or 'butt-dial.'" He pauses. "She changed her mind?"

"What?"

"You said she 'used' to think. She doesn't anymore? Or is she ..." he stops himself. "I'm sorry."

"No, she's not dead," Lexi says. "But she doesn't have a surplus of mind left to change. She has dementia."

"That sucks," Thoreau says. Lexi smiles a little, pleased that Thoreau himself is yet unaware that he's surrendered to the 21st century.

Lexi nods. "I live with her. Sometimes she's great. She's herself. But it's hard not to feel like I'm living with Benjamin Button, you know? A perverse-Benjamin Button. She's becoming a child again, the synapses in her brain snapping apart instead of together."

"Merlin aged in reverse," Thoreau says.

"What?" Lexi asks. If she'd ever learned this before, she'd forgotten it. "Really?"

"I suppose that was different though," Thoreau says. He is about to say more, but another visitor enters—a man carrying a little boy. Lexi is still sitting on the bed and the man looks at her, delighted, perhaps, to find that anything goes in Thoreau's cottage, that this is, in fact, a "please, touch!" museum.

Thoreau turns to the new arrivals. "Greetings," he booms. He is awkward, too loud, as though they've been caught doing something illicit. Lexi supposes that, in a way, they have.

The little boy squirms to be placed on the floor and he is all hands: he wants the book and the pencils on the table, he wants to pull the blanket from the bed.

Lexi wonders if she can wait this party out but decides it is too weird; she's too weird. She stands and sidles to the door. "Thanks, Mr. Thoreau. Sorry if I messed up your house."

"Not at all," Thoreau says, taking a tin cup from the baby's hand. He looks up at her, expectant, perhaps asking for help.

"May the force be with you, or something," Lexi says, trying to smile again. She leaves the house, returning to the bright sunlight and humid air.

***

She follows the signs to the pond, walking down a pounded dirt path through the trees, reviewing her conversation with Thoreau. She forgot herself for a moment, there, with him. She felt as though she could have stayed and talked all day. But did she seem crazy? Maybe. She might have. She is at once intrigued and ashamed; she knows she will think about him and their exchange for the rest of the day, the rest of this trip.

High above, the old trees roll in the wind. Did these same trees see the first Thoreau, the real one, maybe naked, running from his cabin to the lake? And if the original trees are gone, have they told their grandchildren the stories? Do they care to? Do trees, Lexi wonders, have ghosts too?

Walden Pond is big and crowded on this hot day. She finds her group standing awkwardly on the small beach. Lexi realizes, with impatience and a bit of contempt, that despite Dor's instructions, she is the only one to have worn a swimsuit. She nods at Dor but remains at a distance as she strips off her shorts and tee-shirt, leaving them on the gritty orange sand.

She wades in. The water is wonderful, like soft, cool sheets running over bare skin. She swims out, out, out, and then turns back to face the beach she has just left. We human swimmers always do that, she thinks: look back, afraid to lose sight of the land. She dives underneath and when she surfaces, she runs her fingers over her hair, which now feels like silk, like the pelt of a sea mammal. Before she'd passed out the previous night, she'd been watching a nature show. A talking head had claimed, almost off-handedly, that ancient dolphins left the ocean and became land mammals before giving it up and returning again to the sea. This astounded Lexi, and she thinks of it as she treads water, wondering if the dolphins arrived together at a decision to return, and then had inched themselves back to the water, each generation a bit closer. Or had it been a sudden, impulsive, selfish choice: one dolphin, announcing that she'd had enough, she was going back, diving into the waves, and the others, deciding they didn't want to go on without her, following?

When she looks again, she sees Thoreau coming down the path to the lake.

He arrives and stands on the shore. He takes off his hat and squints out at the water. She waves at him, and he waves back.

She swims to the shore, thinking of what she will say to him. He has come to talk to her, hasn't he? She swims fast, half-afraid he'll give up waiting and leave. In the shallow water, she stands and walks, and suddenly she feels great, cinematic, like Brooke Shields in that movie—or was it Bo Derek?—the water running from her fingertips and dripping from her hair as she becomes again substantial.

"Hey," she says.

"It's wonderful, isn't it?" he asks, nodding at the pond.

"Yes," Lexi says.

"I don't mean to interrupt your swim," he says.

"I'm glad you came down," she says. She takes a step closer to him. She feels her group watching them.

"I had a break anyway," he says, so awkward without his character on that she has to fight an impulse to wrap her dripping arms around him and tell him it's all right, she likes him too. "But really I came down to tell you that Merlin said he remembered the future. I thought—I don't know. I felt like that was important. To tell you."

She gasps a little, perhaps from the exertion of the swim, or maybe from the strangeness of him, and of her body, as the drops of water run down from her hair onto her arms, down her back. She says, "Do you want to come over to my hotel tonight and see if we see any ghosts?"

"Yes," he says. "Absolutely."

***

"She's already asleep," Shannon tells Lexi that evening when she calls. "She was going on and on about Ernie. I think she's, like, hallucinating him. Anyway, I took your advice and gave her the CBD."

"That's good."

"And she kept asking me who my kids were. And if you had any kids. She's pretty convinced you've got some, but she couldn't remember their names. Do you have a secret family you're not telling me about?"

"Peanut is my only child," Lexi says knowing this remark will annoy her sister. Before Shannon can respond, though, Lexi tries out the new idea: "Maybe she's remembering the future. Maybe I will have kids someday, and she already knows them."

She hopes Shannon will be intrigued, but Shannon says, "Okay. Whatever," and then returns to her complaints. "She's driving us crazy with the questions. Every five minutes, she asks who Xavier is and when I say he's my husband she raises her eyebrows and suggests he's cheating on me."

"Is he?" Lexi asks.

"Please," Shannon says. "He's too lazy. I suppose he could manage it if I handled the logistics. You know, wrote his dating profile, reminded him to sneak out, picked up the cheap roses ..."

"Well, like I said. Maybe Mom's remembering the future: Xavier surprises everyone and gets off his ass!" Lexi remembers, too late, that there are certain things about which her sister remains un-teasable.

"What the fuck is wrong with you?" Shannon says.

"Sorry," Lexi says. "You're the one who said he was lazy."

"You always take things too far," Shannon snaps. "Why do you always have to say such dumb, stupid things?"

"Dumb and stupid?" Lexi returns. "Someone splurged and got herself a Thesauraus." And then, she adds, again, "Sorry."

But Shannon is not ready to let it go. "You know, you can criticize Xavier all you want, but he's the one baby-sitting your mother so you can go off and enjoy your academic circle jerk."

Lexi can't help but laugh. She imagines the Americanists sitting around, quoting Thoreau and fingering each other. "That's true enough, I guess," she concedes.

***

Lexi wonders who will arrive at her hotel. Will it be Thoreau? Or will it be a weirdo, dressed in a Hooters tee-shirt, or a leather vest, or something else that will repulse her, make clear her horrible mistake? Or, perhaps, he won't come at all.

And so, Lexi is relieved that Thoreau is dressed like a regular 21st-century person: a flannel over a gray tee-shirt, jeans, and the same boots he'd worn earlier. He carries a six-pack of Narragansett beer and a Ouija Board.

"Is that your ghost-hunting equipment?" she asks.

"Yeah," he says, smiling. He holds the beers out. "I heard ghosts like crappy beer."

"Ghosts," Lexi says. "They're just like us."

"Just deader," he returns. "More dead."

***

He tells her his name is Sam. He is twenty-seven. He returned to Concord, his hometown, in May, when he got the job at Walden Pond. He explains that before this, he was the road manager of a band called Doctor Madrid. Lexi hasn't heard of them, but she pulls them up on her phone and they listen to the tinny, raspy music, Lexi sitting on the edge of the bed, Sam across from her on one of the two chairs.

Lexi asks, "So, do you like what you're doing now? Being a Thoreau impersonator?"

Sam shrugs. "I don't usually use the word 'impersonator.' And I love it," he says. "I get to hang out in the cabin all day and be somebody else."

Lexi nods. She understands this. "Yeah," she says. "And you're really good at it. Were you always a big Thoreau fan?"

"Who isn't?" Sam laughs.

Lexi gestures at the Ouija Board. "Should we see if we can find him? Thoreau? Or just go for a generic ghost?"

"Let's shoot for the stars," Sam answers. He picks up the board and joins Lexi on the bed. They both scootch back so that they can lean against the headboard. They put their beers on their respective night tables and sit with the Ouija Board spanning their laps.

"Did you already have a Ouija board or did you pick one up for the occasion?" Lexi asks.

"I knew there was one in the attic of my parent's house. It's my sister's." He runs his fingers over the embossed words: "Parker Brothers."

The hotel décor—old-lady chic, with bulbous lamps and an ancient television perched on an antique dresser—makes Lexi feel as though they are in a home, in someone's childhood bedroom. It makes her feel that she and this Thoreau—this Sam—are at once young together, in a floral-wallpaper past, and here now, too, in the present, in a haunted hotel room in Concord, Massachusetts. She imagines them in other hotel rooms and homes, on other beds, playing other games. She thinks they will get married, maybe, and then she imagines a future that perhaps her mother has already seen: two sweet little boys, close in age, maybe even twins. She sees herself in the car, turning in the driver's seat to see them laughing in the back; she sees them hunched over homework at the dining room table; she sees them watching a movie, their bodies tangled up on the couch.

She imagines telling them about how she had imagined them long before they ever existed.

***

They arrange their damp fingers on the wooden triangle which Google tells them is called a planchette. Lexi pushes her fingertips down to steady her trembling hands.

"Henry David Thoreau? Hello?"

But Thoreau is reticent, perhaps he is put off by their giggling or by his imposter's presence. Or perhaps, Lexi thinks, his line here at the Concord Inn has not been renewed. He has to haunt elsewhere, and part-time.

"Louisa May Alcott?" Sam offers. "Should we see if she's available?"

"Louisa?" Lexi coos, closing her eyes, angling her face toward the ceiling. "Are you there, Louisa? Let us know if you're here."

The planchette jerks and then begins to move slowly across the board.

"You're doing that," Lexi accuses, her eyes squinting open.

"I'm not!" Sam's eyes are also closed, a little smile on his lips.

"F," Lexi says. "Shoot, I should be writing this down." She looks around for a pen and paper, but the planchette will not wait; it swings across the board.

"U," Lexi says.

"C," Sam says. "I wonder where she is going with this."

"Oh, please," Lexi says.

"K," Sam says.

"O," Lexi reads.

The planchette swings to a double-F.

Lexi laughs. "Good for you, Louisa," she says.

***

The six-pack finished, they sit beside each other on the Queen-sized bed.

"Do you think," Lexi asks, "that it's better to never go to therapy at all or to have just a little bit of therapy?"

Sam considers. "I suppose it depends? Did you ever go to therapy?"

"Just a little bit," Lexi concedes.

"Well, was it better than no therapy at all?"

"That's what I'm trying to figure out," Lexi says. She sighs. "I started going because of the whole thing with my mother. It's a real mind fuck, you know? Like, I miss her, but she's right there. And we can have a great conversation, but she won't remember it. It's like talking to a hologram, an AI approximation of my mother. And now, my sister is just dying to put her in a home. So, whatever, I started therapy to talk about that and all the other things that the whole situation brings up. But I would just cry for forty-five minutes and then our time would be over, and I'd still be crying. I'd have to drive home crying. It ruined the rest of the day. I was sort of mad. It felt somehow unethical of my therapist to put me back into the world like that. I felt like I had a sunburn and I was being sent back out to the beach. Naked."

Sam purses his lips and nods. He pats the hand she has resting between them. But he says, "Maybe you could have scheduled your therapy for later in the day?"

Lexi purses her lips. "I suppose. But there's a larger point there."

"I had a great therapist when I was a kid," Sam says. Lexis waits for him to continue, and he says, "I was anxious. I had a lot of anxiety. But my therapist really helped me get it under control."

"That's amazing," Lexi says. "I don't think I have ever heard about anyone for whom therapy was demonstrably successful."

"Well, I'm still anxious," he says.

"You don't seem anxious. You seem really laid back."

Sam shrugs. He moves his hand away and shifts on the bed. "I almost didn't come tonight."

"Really?"

"It was easy to say yes when you were standing right in front of me, dripping all over my boots, but when I went back to the cabin, I was like, what the fuck."

"Oh, God. Did you think I was a psycho or a kidnapper? Or a pedophile? I am thirty-four, you know. I don't know if you knew that."

"No, I didn't think you were a psycho," Sam assures her. "And I don't mind that you're obviously a pedophile. But you did seem a little unhinged. Like, when you got into the bed."

"Unhinged," Lexi laughs. "It's true! I don't know what came over me. I think I momentarily lost my mind."

"Only partly unhinged," he insists. "Mostly kind of cool and interesting."

Lexi smiles. "It can't be easy when you have people like me harassing you at work."

"It can be tough," Sam concedes, bumping her shoulder with his. "When hot older women show up and start jumping in and out of my bed."

"Wait, are you talking about me or do other women do that too?"

"Just the one," Sam says. "Just you."

***

Sam is lovely. He is, Lexi thinks, like a human Xanax. He makes her feel calm and quiet, funnier than she is, cooler than she is. She falls asleep facing him, and she loves it already, the way he smells, underneath the scent of soap and beer and kissing, his human, private, essential smell.

She wakes often, unaccustomed to sleeping next to someone else, but not unhappily. She wakes and thinks about what she will do the next day: she has already told Sam she will blow off the rest of her nerd camp, she will stay, all day, with him at Walden Pond, will leave the cabin only to swim or if she is making other guests uncomfortable. She promises not to get in the bed. At least not when Thoreau has company.

Later she wakes and squints into the darkness, looking for the ghosts. Ernie went through a stage when he would bark at the track lighting in the kitchen. "He must see ghosts," their mother said, but Shannon said it was just the buzz of the lights, probably vibrating at a pitch the humans couldn't hear. When had Shannon gotten so smart? Lexi had said, "Look at you, knowing things."

Maybe her mother really is seeing Ernie, Lexi thinks. Maybe he's returned from her future to keep her company through this part; maybe as we pour out of this life, the next one seeps in a little bit, existential backwash.

Or maybe ghosts are like the dolphins, visible to us only in the breaching, shooting up to take a breath and look around, maybe to remember their old lives on land, just for a moment, before going back, down, away.

BLESSED VIRGIN

Rosemarie recognized her instantly. Any changes were almost totally superficial, as though they were the old Colorforms stick-ons: pink lipstick and big glasses, shoulder-length hair, wrinkles. Peel those away, and there she was again, Sister Grace. Seeing her felt like a punchline, in the best possible way: a relief, a met expectation, a happy twist, and Rosemarie laughed out loud.

Rosemarie blurted, "Sister," and then tried to swallow the "Grace," realizing, too late, her mistake.

The woman turned, clearly taken aback. She squinted and then softened her face. "Is that you, Rosemarie?"

Rosemarie, surprised by sudden tears, gulped, wishing she'd observed a little longer, let the woman come to her, so that, with happy anticipation, she could have watched for that dawning realization, a widening of the eyes behind those surprisingly fashionable black-rimmed glasses.

But calling out to Grace had been irresistible, a reflex, like smelling a baby's head, or digging your toes into the sand, or closing your eyes when you blow out birthday candles.

Rosemarie nodded, mouth open, unable to speak.

Sister Grace stepped closer, her eyes flickering around the room. "I'm not Sister anymore," she said, her smile small and secretive. "I'm just Bernadette Cahill these days."

"Bernadette," Rosemarie whispered.

"Oh, now," Sister Grace said. She put her arms around Rosemarie and embraced her, inhaling deeply. Sister Grace still smelled nice, but it was different, not the same nice that Rosemarie remembered. But, of course, Rosemarie thought. No more convent laundry service, no more sparse dinners with only water to drink, no more abstention from perfumes and lotions, the indulgence of fragrant hair products. Sister Grace was a woman now, again.

The hug felt as though it might go on forever. Gazing over Grace's shoulder, Rosemarie noticed all the buzz and movement around them in the classroom, the new high school freshman and their parents under fluorescent lights, the blurry words of welcome on the whiteboard, the Zora Neale Hurston poster, her jaunty hat and sideways smile. Schools always felt so different at night: safer, warmer, the large, dark windows obscuring the world beyond.

"No one here knows," Sister Grace said into Rosemarie's ear, giving Rosemarie a final squeeze before releasing her. "But it's lovely to see you! What a strange coincidence. Are you ... who's your child?"

"Sophia," Rosemarie said. She nodded her head toward her daughter, slumped against the wall, talking to Jayda, a girl she knew from middle school. Luke, Rosemarie's ex, stood nearby, looking at his phone. "Sophia Williams. Soph, come here," Rosemarie called, trying to make up for in volume what her voice lacked in steadiness. "It's so crazy that you teach here," she said to Sister Grace. "It's so crazy that you're Sophia's English teacher!"

Sophia slouched over, all wary eyes and pouting lips. She scowled at her mother. "What?"

Rosemarie waved a hand toward Sister Grace. "This is, this is, this is—" she began.

"My English teacher?" Sophia said, so bored by her mother's imbecility.

"Sophia," Sister Grace said lightly. "Your mother is simply dumbstruck because I was also her English teacher, all those years ago, at Blessed Virgin."

Sophia failed to react. Sister Grace, accustomed to rude teenagers, soldiered on. "Thank goodness for 'Back-to-School' night, or we might never have figured it out—what with different last names, et cetera. Speaking of, I really should get started—"

"Sister, I mean, Ms. Cahill. Bernadette?" Rosemarie interrupted. If Sophia noticed anything unusual, she didn't show it, at once annoyed and bovine, waiting to be dismissed. "After this—can we go somewhere? Get a cup of coffee?"

"Rosemarie," Sister Grace laughed, looking nervously at Sophia. "I don't think—I have to ..." She cast her eyes around the room, a strained smile on her face, while the other assembled parents shuffled and murmured to each other, impatient and perhaps jealous of the special attention Rosemarie seemed to be getting. "You have my email. We'll plan something for another day? We have so much to catch up on."

"I can't wait," Rosemarie said. And she really couldn't.

***

Rosemarie let herself in the back door and dropped her jacket to the floor.

She congratulated herself on having taken her time getting ready for Back-to-School night. She'd wanted it to be clear to the other new high school parents that she was a cool mom, a stylish mom, a not-obese mom; although she also wished it were known, for the record, that she was absolutely not interested in their stupid husbands, their fat, bald, mean, tired husbands.

It had happened before. At a fundraiser for the elementary school, Rosemarie had slipped out for a smoke with the dad of a kid in Sophia's grade and then next thing she knew, the guy's wife was hustling out there with three friends, agents deployed against interference.

"The guy was fucking disgusting looking," Rosemarie later told her friend Sue. "All of the men our age are."

"Simmer down," Sue had counseled at the time.

No, she wasn't looking for a date, but she still cared, quite a bit, about the opinions of her peers. She thought wryly of her own mother, the way she'd let her hair go gray when she was thirty—thirty!—how she'd oozed into middle age without much more than an occasional dab of Oil of Olay around the eyes.

Rosemarie's daughter, of course, regularly suggested that Rosemarie was repulsive, humiliating, an abomination, and though Rosemarie pretended it didn't sting, it did, terribly. Another one of the indignities of parenthood: finding yourself painfully invested in the opinions of a pimply, fashion-challenged fourteen-year-old.

Rosemarie herself had been a very attractive teenager: lean, with lovely, clear skin that tanned in the summertime (just a hint of red across her cheeks and nose after a day at the beach), and thick, dark, shiny hair. A knockout, her dad used to declare. A true Italian beauty (though she was half-Polish). And she'd not taken her good looks for granted; she'd enjoyed it, all the way up into her thirties when she remained, really, still, very attractive. In her forties, she'd been surprised to find that it didn't matter how pretty you'd previously been. Everything began to sag, to take on new and often startling shapes, lumps materializing in strange places: on the ear lobe, the wrist, the spine. But still, she looked good. It helped to be thin, to have a decent face and a full head of hair. She'd recently remarked to Sue that all the Botox in the world didn't make a difference for some people; no one would notice that your face was as smooth as a baby's ass if you were fat or chinless. Sue, who had also once been a knockout, agreed.

Rosemarie put her keys and bag on the counter and lay down on the kitchen floor with her phone, grateful that Sophia was at her father's.

The cat approached and sniffed, bouncing his cool nose across her cheek before he began to lick her salty face, his tongue reminiscent of an exfoliating treatment Rosemarie had recently endured. He moved down her body and placed one tentative paw and then another on her belly, and, concluding the structure was sound, climbed up and settled down.

Lately, she'd been avoiding the cat, looking at him only out of the corner of her eyes, and she realized, as he kneaded her tummy, that she'd been doing the same to her plants, walking past them the way you drive past a cop, pretending not to notice but watching diligently in your periphery. She realized too, that this was because she felt intense guilt that she never talked to the plants and often forgot to water them; she was afraid that if she made eye contact with her plants they would beseech her to attend to them, to not let them die. She felt badly about it, but not badly enough to bestir herself to water them.

She lifted her phone into the air in front of her face. She googled "Bernadette Cahill."

And there was Sister Grace, that same professional smile she used in her Blessed Virgin yearbook faculty photo, her head tilted sideways, her bright eyes laughing.

When Rosemarie was a junior, she would have lunch in Sister Grace's office every Tuesday, ostensibly to discuss Rosemarie's college applications. But the conversations always drifted into poetry and novels and movies, and then perhaps to Rosemarie's parents, and Rosemarie's friends, Rosemarie's boyfriend, Rosemarie's part-time job. After she'd left each Tuesday, Rosemarie would take that conversation and replay it in her head for the rest of the week, smiling to herself as she remembered clever remarks she'd made, or cringing at the dumb, awkward things she'd said, the jokes that didn't land or the ideas she couldn't quite communicate. She'd review it again and again until she'd exhausted it and then she would begin planning out what she would say the coming Tuesday, with what anecdotes she would delight and concern and enthrall her pretty teacher.

"My mother reached up my skirt," she once told Sister Grace. "She said it was too short and then she cornered me and literally put her hand up my skirt and grabbed my vagina and said that this was what boys would do to me." She watched for Sister Grace's reaction; the teacher blinked rapidly. "It was basically child abuse," Rosemarie continued. "But I don't care. I went upstairs to change and then I just stuck the skirt in my bag and put it back on in the driveway."

"Rosemarie," Sister Grace had clucked disapprovingly. Still, Rosemarie could tell she was impressed.

Rosemarie missed Sister Grace over the long summer before senior year—the vacation only six weeks, but feeling at once endless and accelerated—as Rosemarie ricocheted from late nights in dive bars to her job at the counter of a pizza place to ever-more horrible arguments with her mother, her mother, who told Rosemarie that if she didn't watch it, she would slap her face right off, a threat that conjured for Rosemarie an image of herself as faceless and compliant, perhaps precisely the daughter her mother had always wanted.

That fall, Rosemarie and Sister Grace continued their weekly lunches, even after the applications had been submitted and even though, as a senior, Rosemarie was allowed to leave campus for lunch and could have gone, really, anywhere, with her friends, who teased her and called her a kiss up and a nerd. The teasing didn't get any traction though because it never bothered Rosemarie at all. Because Rosemarie knew they were jealous because Sister Grace was young and funny and beautiful and, of all the girls at Blessed Virgin, had chosen her.

***

She was about to put the phone down when she saw she had a new email.

What a surprise to see you tonight, Rosemarie. It's been a long time. As I suggested when we spoke, I don't share my history in religious life with my students. Most of my colleagues don't know either. I would never ask you to lie, but I would like to continue to be discreet. Not everyone has fond memories of nuns, if you know what I mean. Of course, please feel free to tell people that I was your teacher, back when you were in high school. Although that does make me feel old. I was just a kid then too, though, really. I was twenty-three when I started teaching at Blessed Virgin! Twenty-four, twenty-five when I knew you.

I've enjoyed teaching here at West and I look forward to working with your daughter. If she's half as talented as her mother, I'm sure she will go far. What are you doing these days? Do you still write? I hope so.

All my love,
Bernadette

All my love, Rosemarie thought.
All my love all my love all my love.
All of it?

***

Lesbians had a pop culture moment in the 1990s, albeit a fraught, semi-exploitative, and often sexist one. And Blessed Virgin was still a Catholic school in Queens, and the students there were mean, mostly narrow-minded teenagers. So when a girl named Christina in Rosemarie's year announced that she was gay, she was immediately, cruelly, and relentlessly harassed. Someone started calling her Christuna—a vulgar joke that only revealed the mean girl's own internalized misogyny—and it stuck.

Christuna was curly-haired, sullen, and awkwardly big-busted, the space between each button of her uniform shirt straining and gapping. She'd not been on Rosemarie's radar, really, until she'd "come out." It had seemed so ridiculous, so self-important and attention-seeking, that it struck Rosemarie as sort of pathetic and made her angry, even, although she couldn't quite articulate why. And then Sister Grace had mentioned the other girl, had quoted some St. Francis of Assisi at Rosemarie, and said, "Some of the girls are giving Christina Cassella a hard time. Maybe you'll keep an eye out for her." What did Sister Grace know about it, Rosemarie had wondered.

Though she'd said, "yes, of course, Sister," and Grace had made some remark about Rosemarie being a shining light for the others (which Rosemarie enjoyed and turned over in her mind for a long time after), the fact that Christuna had run off to complain to Sister Grace filled Rosemarie with a weird possessiveness that, if she were being honest, recalled for her the way Rosemary's father overreacted—seemed to take it personally—when someone parked in the spot in front of their narrow house.

It was years later, wryly aware of the complete surrender to demographic conformity, that Rosemarie drank wine on the front porch of her own wide suburban home (overnight parking not even permitted in Glen Harbor), talking to her friend Sue, that Rosemarie remembered Christuna. She'd been telling Sue about Blessed Virgin, and Sue, who knew that Rosemarie had lived with a woman before marrying a man, asked if it had been delightfully ironic that her conservative parents sent her to an all-girls school.

Rosemarie shook her head, no. She said, "I had crushes on girls, but I only dated boys. I wasn't that self-aware. Being a lesbian wasn't really an option—an imaginable possibility—for me. I mean, you know Big Ron and Paulina." Rosemarie was about to make a face to suggest her parents' overall absurdity as human beings, but had to stop talking because she suddenly recalled that none of what she was saying was true. She thought of Grace. And then she thought of Christuna. "There was … well. There was one girl," she said.

"Go on," Sue said, swirling the wine in her glass to suggest she was intrigued.

"Fuck," Rosemarie said. "I forgot about Christuna. Jesus, I suppose I was really self-hating." She ducked her head and closed her eyes, as if she could un-summon the memory.

"Christuna? Now you have to tell me," Sue said.

"You'll hate me," Rosemarie said.

"Nothing could make me hate you," Sue said, scooting a little closer in her rattan chair. "Except maybe not telling me this story."

***

Poor Christuna; Rosemarie remembered her cautious eyes, her quivering lip.

"Just because I like girls doesn't mean I want to hook up with *you*," Christuna had said snootily, backing up into the radiator, into the sweet-smelling hissing heat.

"I just think you're so pretty," Rosemarie had countered. "And cool." She shrugged a little, nodded her head encouragingly. "Don't be a tease." These were the exact words that a boy had used on Rosemarie herself the previous weekend, words that had worked their magic, had roused in her an irresistible desire not to kiss him, but to remain in his esteem. And Rosemarie recognized the look on Christuna's face too, an expression of doubt but also a guarded interest, a longing to hear more nice things, that battled with her impulse to flee.

Rosemarie hadn't planned the encounter; she'd simply come across the other girl alone in the bathroom. But her movement toward Christuna had also felt irresistible, a thrilling surrender, like righteous anger. What had Sister Grace wanted her to do? "Where there is hatred sow love?" It occurred vaguely to Rosemarie that this wasn't at all what Grace had meant, but, oh well.

Despite her initial protests, Christuna almost immediately relented, allowing Rosemarie to stuff her into a stall, to kiss her sloppily and feel her up, ungently, and then even stick her hand down Christuna's skirt, under her tights, under her underwear.

That's what Rosemarie was doing, feverishly, when the nuns, tipped off, barged in, not unlike that gang of moms Rosemarie would encounter at the fundraiser years later, the nuns pounding on the door so that the whole bank of stalls shook, shouting, "That's enough now, girls. Come right out."

The nuns. They were always so worried about the boys, of what the boys might do, of what the boys might get the girls to do. They were confounded by this new trend of girls doing things to other girls. Or at least they pretended to be.

***

"Poor Christuna," Sue had said. "You realize that you're basically a rapist."

"That's not funny," Rosemarie whimpered, shrinking into her chair. "I feel terrible about it. But I didn't force her. Maybe I persuaded her. Maybe I was coercive. But I feel like all sex was coercive back then. Wasn't it?"

"So then what happened?" Sue asked, uninterested in quibbling.

"I already told you," Rosemarie shook her head. "Some tattletale must have come in and realized what was going on and went and got the nuns. They burst in before things could go any farther. Further?"

"But did you get in trouble?"

"Not really. The principal, Sister Charles, called my parents."

Sue widened her eyes. "I can only imagine how Paulina and Big Ron reacted to finding out their daughter was fingering girls in the bathroom of Our Lady of the Bleeding Womb."

"Blessed Virgin. Our Lady Blessed Virgin. Sister Charles was mercifully vague," Rosemarie said. "The phrase she used with my parents was 'inappropriate experimentation.' I know this because my mother repeated it to me. Paulina and Big Ron willfully misunderstood it to mean smoking or maybe marijuana. So it was fine."

"So nothing bad happened to you."

"It was a confusing time," Rosemarie protested. "I mean, I was scared."

"What happened to Christuna?"

***

Twenty-four, twenty-five when I knew you.

She'd put that in on purpose, Rosemarie thought. She always said I was a good close-reader, that I never missed a trick. This reference to age was a hint, a reminder. It told Rosemarie: *I wasn't that much older than you; what's seven years?*

What's seven years when she's not your teacher, when she's not a nun? What's seven years?

On her kitchen floor, Rosemarie watched a mosquito—one impossibly long, wire-like limb extended—bumping blindly along the ceiling. She wanted to get up and kill the bug, but she hated to disturb the cat, who was humming along happily on her chest. This was the most contact and attention he'd gotten in days. Rosemarie had read that pet-ownership decreased blood pressure, helped you deal with stress, and yet Rosemarie felt the cat was one of her primary sources of low-grade anxiety. She often felt the cat was trying to communicate with her; the cat, who pooped in the long-suffering potted plants. But what, besides the fact that he wanted his litter scooped more often, could he possibly have to tell her?

She read Sister Grace's message again. And then, holding the phone awkwardly and close to her face, she wrote, "Coffee tomorrow? I'm free after 5:00."

Sister Grace. Sister What-a-Waste, they'd called her because she was so pretty. Pretty girls only became nuns in the movies or in Africa, in Rosemarie's experience. Pretty Irish girls from Brooklyn, girls with cute, freckled noses and light gray eyes and upper lips that met like two hands folded together in prayer: they might be devout, but they didn't become nuns. Those days were long gone, even back in the 90s.

Rosemarie tried to remember. She'd asked, comfortable in the warm classroom, the rain outside making Rosemarie feel calm and sleepy, "Why did you become a nun?"

Sister Grace had been quiet, her eyes falling out of focus in such a way as to make Rosemarie think that Sister Grace must have been one of those people who, riding the subway or taking out the trash or praying the rosary, had heard God's voice calling to her, clear like a solitary gull's cry at the empty beach. But Sister Grace said, her voice low and gravelly and full of pain, "I had to get away from my family." And then she'd smiled at Rosemarie, that same, sad, closed-lipped smile. "The sisters took me in."

Rosemarie wanted to know why, what had her family done to her? Why not just get a job at Burger King, save up, and move out? Why go to such lengths? But she perhaps already knew: it was what all of their families were like, wasn't it, only different in degree? Rosemarie wanted to cry, then, thinking of Grace, thinking of how bad it must have been for her to run away to the nuns.

Rosemarie asked, "How old were you?"

"About your age."

"Are you glad you joined?"

Sister Grace thought for a moment and then looked at the window, streaked with rain. "Most of the time, yes."

"I wish I had known you," Rosemarie said, impulsively. "Back then. I wish I could have … helped. If I had known you then."

"You have such a good heart," Sister Grace said, still looking out the window.

And then, even more impulsively, Rosemarie inclined toward Sister Grace, her hand crawling across the desk that separated them, her index finger extended, stretching toward Grace, like the bodiless hand of a horror movie, or like a plant tendril reaching for the sun. When it arrived at Grace, Rosemarie ran her finger down the length of Grace's wrist, down over the top of her hand, stopping at the tip of Grace's finger.

Rosemarie remembered: Grace had shivered.

And then Sister Grace rose, the chair making a terrible, scraping noise as she pushed herself out. She walked to the window. Her cheeks, already so hollow, looked deeply shadowed, her eyes pained. With longing? Rosemarie wondered. Or disgust?

"I'm sorry, Rosemarie," Sister Grace looking out at the wet, gray streets. "I have so much work to do today. Maybe ... next week? We can pick out something to read over the Christmas break."

***

It was the following Tuesday that, instead of having lunch with Sister Grace, Rosemarie had preyed upon Christuna. And it was only then, that night lying on the kitchen floor, that Rosemarie even made the connection. She almost laughed, thinking of it, it was so obvious. It was like hearing someone else's dream about rotten teeth or falling elevators or un-dialable phones.

Instead of going to see Sister Grace the following Tuesday and acting like everything was normal and nothing had changed, she'd cornered Christuna in the bathroom.

Rosemarie wondered what else she was hiding from herself.

"Did she get in trouble too?" Sue had asked the night they'd gotten drunk on the front porch. "Christuna? What happened to her?" Rosemarie thought that Sue, whose own young adulthood had been a Rube Goldberg-machine of disasters, with Sue herself the marble rolling ineluctably toward each ruinous choice and its attendant destruction, was maybe enjoying the story a little too much. Well, let her, Rosemarie thought. She knew two things for sure about her friend. The first was that rather than transforming from a troubled youth to a judgmental adult, she'd traveled in the opposite direction, developing an expansive empathy, despite her sometimes too-cutting humor. And second, Sue was incredibly, unfailingly, sometimes irrationally, loyal. She'd forgive Rosemarie pretty much anything—something Rosemarie had experienced first-hand.

"Things didn't work out so well for her," Rosemarie said.

"Why? What happened?"

"I suppose I wasn't very nice."

"What did you do?"

"She tried to tell people, you know, that something had happened between us. As though that would help her, maybe earn her some popularity points or something. But I told everyone that I was just trying to be nice to her and that she, like, assaulted me." Rosemarie grimaced. "Everyone thought she was totally gross and pathetic. God, I was such a bitch."

"Poor Christuna."

"She wound up changing schools." Rosemarie said. She didn't remember much about Christuna after that one eventful day, but she did remember sneering, and she did remember her proxies, calling Christuna a pervert, saying, "I have to go home and shower. Christuna just underessed me with her eyes." There might have been some shoving, some theft of personal property. "I mean, it wasn't anything too terrible, I don't think," Rosemarie

Dirty Suburbia

clarified to Sue. She found herself using Grace's words: "I think some of the girls, you know, gave her a hard time." She cleared her throat. "And then, one day, we noticed she wasn't there anymore. She sort of just slipped the scene. Maybe she went to public school. Good for her, I guess?"

"Poor Christuna," Sue had said again. She paused and added, "Don't you think it's about time to stop calling her Christuna?"

"Yeah," Rosemarie said. "You're probably right."

***

The Tuesdays marched on: there was the Tuesday with Christuna in the bathroom, and then suddenly it was Christmas, and then the Tuesday after break was "Ring Day" and the seniors all went out for lunch. Rosemarie couldn't remember if Christuna had been there, at the Ring Day celebration, taking pictures under a balloon arch in the cafeteria. She didn't think so. She thought that maybe Christuna was already gone by then.

Rosemarie had thought about Sister Grace constantly, and especially on Tuesdays, with a pang of longing and remorse. She wished she hadn't blown it, acted so rashly, so passionately, even. She'd seen Grace in the hallways a few times—had even once seen Grace walking with Christuna before Christuna disappeared—and had always ducked into the bathroom or locked her eyes on her companion, pretending not to see Grace. She cycled through feeling so ashamed that she thought she might literally die, and then feeling a bit indignant that Grace wasn't lovesick, missing her, obviously dying of want, before descending into a familiar regret, the impotent sadness of a child who longs for a do-over.

But then, in Math one day, a sophomore entered the classroom and padded silently to where Mr. McClellan sat grading exams. The girl handed him a note and he squinted up at his students, still not sure who was who, even this late in the year: "Rosemarie, Sister Livia Dennis has asked for you in Room 222. Bring your things."

Rosemarie's friends snickered and Rosemarie rolled her eyes. Sister Living Dead should have been retired long ago but instead served as a glorified hallway monitor who specialized in uniform infractions. The girls joked that she relished the chance to tuck your skirt in for you, copping a feel under the pretense of making sure she got it in there nice and tight.

But when Rosemarie pushed open the heavy door, there was Grace, alone in the empty classroom, standing by the window. "I'm sorry for the subterfuge," Grace said, her face drawn and worried. "They wouldn't like—I can't—I don't know where to begin." Rosemarie had never before seen someone literally wring their hands.

Had a catastrophe occurred? Had she heard about what Rosemarie had done to Christuna? Was she upset? Jealous, even?

"Please," Rosemarie said, flipping her hair over her shoulder and dropping her backpack to a desk with a clunk, pretending nonchalance but unable to swallow the quaver in her voice. "I was about to stab myself with a protractor just to get out of there."

"Rosemarie," Grace said, not acknowledging the remark. "A lot has happened these past few weeks." She shook her head, several, quick, small shakes, as though responding to a voice Rosemarie couldn't hear. Rosemarie wished she hadn't come. She didn't like to see Grace like this. And yet she took a step closer as Grace continued, "I'm leaving Blessed Virgin."

"What?"

"It's complicated," Sister Grace said. "But I want you to know that it has nothing to do with you. I wanted you to know that. I wanted to take this opportunity to wish you all the best, dear Rosemarie. I hope that you'll always remember that you are one of God's children, that His light is in you too, that you will follow your better instincts, your instincts toward kindness and—"

"No," Rosemarie said simply. It was her turn to shake her head. "Is this about—"

And then Grace was beside her, a hand on her shoulder.

"Oh, Rosemarie. Don't cry. Please don't cry."

Rosemarie could smell her: talcum powder and unshaven armpits under damp polyester. She let herself be embraced, and she rested her cheek against Grace's cool cheek, her eyes closed, inhaling. "You're a good person, Rosemarie," Grace was saying when Rosemarie turned her head, just slightly, just the smallest bit, and her lips were on Grace's face and then on Grace's mouth.

Grace stepped back and away, though she took Rosemarie's sweaty hand in her own. "Oh, no, Rosemarie. No, no, no." Rosemarie saw her red eyes were wet. "Oh, Rosemarie," she said.

Sister Grace said something else, but Rosemarie wasn't listening. She stared over Grace's shoulder, looking at the plaster statue of the Virgin Mary above the chalkboard, the pale-skinned Mary in her bright blue gown, her cheeks and lips pink, the ideal woman of an earlier era.

***

Rosemarie checked her phone. There was no reply.

She had loved Sister Grace, she thought. She had been in love with her, even if she'd been young, just a teenager. Just a few years older than Sophia.

Rosemarie never saw her again at Blessed Virgin. Rosemarie walked in the next day and didn't have to be told; she could feel Grace's absence, the building too hot, suffocating, and too small without her in it. And then, the day after that, Kerry, Rosemarie's best friend at the time, told their lunch table that her mother, who was friends with Sister Charles's niece, had told her that Sister Grace had been transferred because someone had complained that there had been some sort of inappropriate relationship with a student.

"Inappropriate?" Rosemarie had choked. She remembered: she was eating bright orange cheese-flavored popcorn and a sharp piece had stuck in her throat. She'd gulped milk from a carton to try and wash it down, but the kernel lodged there, unmoveable. "What?"

"Oh, I know you love her," Kerry said, rolling her eyes. "But you have to admit she does give off some weird lesbo vibes."

"Inappropriate? How?" Rosemarie said again. "Who complained?"

Kerry smirked. "Was it you, Rosemarie?" She grabbed another girl, Araceli, by the shoulders. "Show us on the doll where she touched you."

"I just can't believe it," Rosemarie had said, trying to mask her distress as disbelief, as genuine curiosity. "I just wonder who complained."

"Whatever," Kerry had said. "The nuns and priests are all fucking dykes and pedophiles anyway."

***

Finally, a new message.

Sister Grace had replied. She would meet Rosemarie at Deep Roots, a coffee shop near the school, the next evening. She was so looking forward to it.

***

The cat was sent skittering across the kitchen. Rosemarie buzzed around the house with renewed purpose, moving automatically as she fantasized about the meeting at the coffee shop, about an instant rekindling, the recovery of a connection never truly severed. She would be bold; she would bring up the kiss. She would tell Grace how angry she was and how disgusted she'd been at the time with whoever had suggested their relationship was "inappropriate," how she'd never known for sure who had done it, but how Grace's leaving, her literal dis-grace, had been a source of pain for years, like an undiagnosed but chronic condition, invisible to others, but disruptive and acute nevertheless.

She texted Luke—could Sophia stay again at his place tomorrow? She was being presumptuous, but still. She didn't want to take things slow with Grace; things had been slow enough already. It occurred to her that it was possible that Grace was still a virgin. A true blessed virgin! There were those years in the convent, and, after she left, probably several years of wrestling with her sexuality; even if she didn't identify as a lesbian or as bi, she had been a devout Catholic and God knows what that'll do to a woman. Rosemarie thrilled to the idea of being the one to introduce Grace to this other, new, exquisite world. She was younger than Grace, but she'd always been, in some ways, she thought, more worldly. Rosemarie imagined shocking, thrilling, enthralling her teacher, just like in the old days.

Driving to work in the still-dark morning, her lips moved as she imagined telling her best friend Sue about Grace. She imagined Grace, too, telling people about how tragic it had been when they'd been separated, about how beautiful Rosemarie had been (although she's even more beautiful now, Grace might add), about how their reunion didn't even feel that surprising, because Grace had always known they'd come back to each other.

They'd have one of those fantastic, gorgeous, ridiculously expensive weddings, the kind you can only really have when you're older because you finally have some money and more importantly, some taste, and even sour Sophia would be happy. Her skin would have cleared up and they'd do a picture of the three of them wearing crowns of flowers, Sophia standing between Rosemarie and Grace. The photographer would remark that Sophia and Rosemarie could be sisters.

***

And then, there she was, the bell above the door tinkling as she entered Deep Roots, Grace so clearly a lesbian that Rosemarie laughed out loud. She should have given Kerry more credit.

"Rosemarie," Sister Grace said.

"I'm so happy to see you," Rosemarie said, rising awkwardly, leaning in for a hug across the table, and then sitting down again when Grace, also awkwardly, excused herself to go to the counter for a coffee.

Rosemarie pretended to look at her phone, her mind buzzing, careening from the classroom at Blessed Virgin to this comfortable coffee shop, from the days of Grace's soft, unlined cheek and polyester-blend blouses to today's Patagonia fleece, her lip-glossed lips.

"I have to talk to you about something," Rosemarie said as soon as Grace sat down across from her, knowing that her intensity could be frightening, knowing that she should ease into it, but unable to resist. "Grace. Bernadette, God, I've wanted to talk to you for years."

Sister Grace leaned her head forward, widening her eyes slightly. She looked at once alarmed and amused, just like the old days, as if whatever it was Rosemarie might say promised to be shocking, but most certainly still charming, disarming, delightful.

"It wasn't me," Rosemarie said. "I know when you left—they said someone had complained, had suggested that—how did they phrase it? That there was something 'inappropriate' going on. It wasn't me. I don't know who it was. Maybe somebody saw us—"

"I know," Grace tried to interrupt. "Rosemarie—"

"I always worried that you might think it was me, that you might have thought that I—and I would never have—I always wanted, I think you knew, I think you were aware of how I felt and," Rosemarie couldn't get it out, it was stuck somehow, and she thought again of the popcorn kernel. She cleared her throat.

"I know," Grace said, not smiling. She raised her hand and waved it back and forth as she spoke and then Rosemarie saw it: a wedding band. "It was awful, of course. The end of my time at Blessed Virgin—it was incredibly painful for me. I became deeply depressed. I questioned everything. And I wound up leaving religious life altogether. Of course, I can see now that leaving was the right thing to do. And I've been very happy, honestly—"

"But who told them?" Rosemarie interrupted, no longer as breathless, her voice now a bit deeper, angrier. That Grace was married was not an insurmountable obstacle, but the fact annoyed Rosemarie. She ran a finger over her already-smooth forehead, smiled, flipped her hair back over her shoulder, and leaned, she hoped fetchingly, toward Grace. "How did they find out?"

Grace looked at her for a long moment, and Rosemarie wondered if she was being admired. But then Grace said, "It was Christina's parents, of course. I suppose I thought you knew. I thought everyone knew." She sniffed and then smiled sadly. She must have registered Rosemarie's lack of understanding because she added, "Christina Casella."

"Christina Casella," Rosemarie repeated, shaking her head.

"You know Christina," Grace said. She made a face that seemed, to Rosemarie, to express exasperation, disbelief. "She was in your class."

Rosemarie clenched her jaw in an attempt to get some control over her own face. She picked up her coffee and then noticed her hand was shaking—her veiny, middle-aged, well-moisturized hand—and so she put the coffee back down again without drinking.

"We used to call her Christuna," Rosemarie said.

"I know," Grace said. She shook her head. "You treated her very badly."

"I didn't—she was the one who …" Rosemarie began. "But what does that have to do with you? With us?"

It was Grace's turn to shake her head. "You and I? It wasn't about … 'us.' Christina's parents found our letters. Letters between Christina and myself. And then we were on the phone one night and we didn't know it, but her mother was listening. She had picked up the line in their bedroom, and … it was actually quite innocent but what she heard … upset her." Grace smiled down into her tea. "A lot of unspoken longing. Perhaps not appropriate. But, as I said, innocent. Honestly, nothing happened while I was still at Blessed Virgin." Grace said. "I'm so sorry. I can see that you're shocked. I really thought you knew. I thought everyone knew. We're married now," she continued. "Christina and I have been married for almost twenty years!"

Grace smiled, then, those perfect pink lips closed and twisting up, those same lips but now with tiny, lovely parenthesis, wrinkles from years of laughing, her gray eyes, flecked with yellow, not laughing now.

"She sends her regards," Grace said. "My sweet Christina. I asked her to join us, but, you know. She hasn't really gotten over all of it." Grace stopped smiling. She wrinkled her nose. "What you did to her was vicious," she said so gently, it took Rosemarie a moment to understand.

Rosemarie made a choking noise and raised her hand to her throat. She turned her face away and saw the two of them reflected in the darkened window. She looked, she thought, so lovely like this, in the dim, obscure, soft light.

"But tell me," Grace continued soothingly. "Tell me how you've been. Tell me all about Rosemarie, just like you used to."

Rosemarie couldn't unstick her gaze from the window, but Grace met her eye in the reflection.

"Vicious," Rosemarie repeated, as though to practice her pronunciation, as though she were learning a new language, now, at her age.

NOT FOR EVERYONE

The problems seemed to start on the afternoon of Christmas Eve. Joanne's mother had run out for some forgotten celery and seen a penis at the grocery store.

"A phallus," she reported, her face drained of color. "At Fresh Country Farms." She gently placed her grocery totes on the floor by the front door. "An enormous, gray..." She shuddered.

Joanne and her father, on the living room sofa, both looked up from their phones.

Joanne's first thought was that her mother, perhaps, did not understand the definition of the word *phallus*. "Mom, what are you talking about?" she asked, sitting up straighter. She looked at her father. "What is she talking about?"

"It sounds like she's talking about penises," her father answered. He returned to his phone. "But your guess is as good as mine."

Her mother sank into the armchair next to the couch.

"Did someone ... expose himself to you?" Joanne asked. Her mother shook her head, no, and unbuttoned her winter coat. It was unseasonably mild, and Joanne could see sweat on her mother's upper lip.

"No," her mother said. "Yes. It was on the screen."

"The screen?"

"The flat-screen TV. Above the checkout, where they display, you know, the specials and sales. I was looking at a picture of navel oranges one minute and then this ... phallus," she used that obfuscating word, again, sort of infuriatingly, "appeared on the screen. It was ... engorged. It looked ... unwell. There was a hand holding it. Clutching it." Her mother's lips turned down in prim disgust.

Joanne looked around the room, as if for confirmation that this conversation was really happening. Her father didn't look up. "What did you do?" Joanne asked.

Her mother raised her hands in the air limply, a gesture of defeat. "No one else seemed to notice. By the time I thought to tell anyone, the screen had changed. I was in shock. I paid for my things and came straight home. I couldn't believe it. I still can't believe it."

"Could it have been, like, a zucchini or something?"

Her mother regarded her coldly. "I know what I saw."

"Well, that's very bizarre."

"It's more than bizarre!"

"Okay, but, you know, no one was hurt." Joanne leaned back into the couch.

"I was hurt," her mother declared, suddenly tearful. "I was hurt. I didn't want to see that."

"Okay," Joanne reasoned gently. "I get that. But, you know, it was just a picture."

Her mother's lips curled down, as though Joanne herself had inflicted the penis upon her. "I thought you were a feminist," she said bitterly.

To this, Joanne had no ready response. "I am," she said carefully. She might have added that it was precisely her feminism that would have rendered the appearance of a "phallus" in a surprising location a little less of a psychic blow than it appeared to be to her mother, but instead, she blinked a few times and then turned again to her father for help.

Her father, however, was busy smiling at something he was reading on the Internet.

Sensing eyes on him, he asked, "How does AOC define a racist?"

"Not now, Dad," Joanne groaned.

"First you have to be white."

"Dad."

"And second, you have to disagree with her. First one is totally optional, though."

Joanne shook her head. "Not the right time, Dad."

"I've got another one."

"Dad!" Joanne shouted. "Mom is really upset!"

Her father looked at her mother. "Calm down, Marcy. I doubt you saw what you think you saw. Sometimes a zucchini is just a zucchini."

"You," her mother began, standing. Joanne saw that she was trembling. "You …" She inhaled sharply before turning and marching from the room.

"Dad," Joanne said again.

He had returned to his screen. "Don't worry, Jo. She's just anxious about Christmas and Timmy's arrival and all that."

Joanne considered. "She actually seemed pretty upset. And angry with you," she observed.

"Meh. That's baked-in resentment," her dad returned. "That's nothing new."

***

Joanne's brother Tim and his wife Katrina and their son Adam arrived about an hour later, annoyed. There had been traffic, of course, and everyone reported feeling carsick, but it also turned out that they had skipped lunch and were starving. When Joanne asked, "Hangry?" and no one even rolled their eyes good-naturedly, she thought, but did not say, "quod erat demonstrandum."

Meanwhile, Joanne's mother seemed to have mostly recovered, but she was shrill and over-excited by Tim's family's arrival, touching them and trying to take things from their hands and standing too close, while they visibly shrank from her. Then, when Adam sat down for dinner without taking his eyes off his iPad, Joanne watched as her mother's own eyes widened with alarm.

"You don't let him bring it to the table?" she asked.

"Just tonight," Tim said. "He'll be bored otherwise."

"But it's Christmas Eve!" Joanne's mother protested.

"It makes life easier," Tim reasoned. "Relax, Mom. I'll tell him he can't have it at dinner tomorrow."

"I just sent you something," Joanne's father announced, entering from the kitchen and carrying a bowl of mashed potatoes. "Check your phone, Tim."

"Is it another Alexandria Ocasio-Cortez gif?" Tim asked.

"It sure is."

"Jesus, Dad," Tim said.

"Dad, you're obsessed with her," Joanne put in, sensing an ally.

"She's comedy gold," Joanne's father returned. "She's such a moron."

"I don't think she's a moron," Joanne said evenly, straining not to betray her true feelings for the politician, whom she had met once at a "St. Pat's For All" celebration in Queens. AOC was as luminous and red-lipsticked in person as she was on Twitter, and she was so gracious about taking a photo with Joanne that Joanne had almost felt as if it had been AOC's idea to begin with. Then, when Joanne had posted the picture and tagged AOC, AOC had commented with a heart emoji, earning Joanne's undying, unshakeable devotion.

Even though this had all happened before her father had developed his obsession, Joanne had never mentioned it to her family, and now, if she were to mention that she'd met AOC, it might seem as though she were deliberately baiting her father, or as though her admiration of AOC was a rejection of him, which, Joanne felt, would be a somewhat self-involved misinterpretation. Although, she wondered at the table, was it possible that the reverse was true: that her father's hatred of AOC was some sort of subconscious, preemptive rejection of Joanne? She resolved to consider this more fully later.

"Please," Joanne's mother said. "No politics at the table."

"It's not politics, Marcy," Joanne's father said. "It's entertainment."

Joanne's mother harrumphed and repositioned a platter of meat. "I think we're ready. Mike, will you lead us in a prayer?"

"All right," her father barked. "Let's pray. Adam, put away that goddamn Gameboy."

Joanne laughed, and Adam peered up warily, unclear as to what was funny. Katrina snatched the iPad from her son's hands, flipping the cover shut. "You'll get it back later," she hissed.

Joanne's father said a few words about gratitude and family and Christmas. Then he added, "And Lord, we thank you for Donald Trump. He may be from Queens, but he is from Queens when Queens was Long Island and Long Island was the countryside, before Queens was surrendered completely to the unwashed masses."

"Dad," Joanne groaned.

"What?" her father asked, unclasping his prayer hands. "Are we going to have to move to Suffolk next?"

"Just ignore him," Joanne's mother said preemptively. She passed the Joanne the potatoes.

"That's right, that's what you should do, just keep ignoring the white male," her father warned. "We've never contributed anything to society."

"How's school?" Joanne asked Adam, trying to take her mother's advice. "Do you like your teacher?"

"Yeah," Adam answered. His eyes darted to his father. "Can I have the iPad back now?"

"No. Eat something," Tim answered through gritted teeth.

"He's addicted to that goddamn thing," Joanne's father said. "Kids today." He smirked and picked up his own phone. "Have I shown you this one yet?" he turned his phone around to display an image of, who else?, AOC, mid-laugh. Joanne couldn't read the text; she shook her head and turned to her sister-in-law.

"So, what's going on with you, Katrina?" Joanne asked.

Katrina was child-sized and blonde and had long, thin fingers on which she wore huge, sparkling rings. She'd been gazing at her food with a vague, disturbed smile, but she looked up and answered, "Oh, everything's great," before deflecting, "How's school for you?"

"It was a good semester," Joanne answered. "I won the award for best grad student essay."

"That's great." Katrina smiled tightly.

Joanne waited for someone to ask what the essay was about. She had on deck what she believed was an amusing anecdote, but Katrina, instead, asked: "And you teach the one course?"

Joanne nodded. "Yup. Just the one." This was a source of amusement to her father, she knew, who asked her what she did with the rest of her time. He did not seem to believe or to understand that she wrote and researched in addition to grading and preparing for class. And perhaps because she never did write or research or prepare as much as she really should, his suggestions that she was somehow slacking left her feeling at once enraged and abashed, feeling misunderstood and, perhaps, understood a bit too acutely.

"Just the one," Joanne repeated. "But you know. It's like a goldfish. You put a goldfish in a big bowl and it will grow to be enormous. Somehow the teaching is like a goldfish. It winds up eating all my time."

"Looks like you've been doing quite a bit of eating yourself," her father joked, chewing jauntily.

Joanne looked at her plate, the pain like a stubbed toe when you're walking home from the beach: infuriating, but not unexpected. Your own fault, maybe, really.

"Not nice, Mike," Joanne's mother said.

"Anyway, I have wonderful students," Joanne said to no one in particular.

You can't argue with someone who calls you fat, Joanne had learned. If you protested, they'd tell you that you were in denial. If you said that you knew you were fat, but didn't think that was such a bad thing, they would still tell you that you were in denial.

She wasn't in denial. Which is not to say that she'd not been unastonished when she'd stepped on the scale in her parent's bathroom. Her father was right; she had gained weight. According to an app on her phone, she was now obese, and not in the, "I'm-'technically'-obese, but-even-Tom-Cruise-is-considered-obese-according-to-the-way-they-figure-these-things, isn't it-ridiculous?" kind of way.

Despite this, she loved her body. In fact, when she checked herself out in the mirror, she often thought, wow, I look amazing.

Perhaps she had reverse-anorexia of some sort, a kind of anorexia that made you think you were skinnier or more attractive than you actually were. An excess of self-confidence. A surplus of self-love.

And regardless of what her family thought, Joanne had found that plenty of other people had thought she looked amazing too.

She scooped and plopped a mound of mashed potatoes on her plate.

"So, someone put a picture of a penis on the flat-screen TV at Fresh Country Farms and it freaked mom out," she said.

"What?" Tim asked.

"Joanne!" her mother cried, putting her fork down angrily. "There are children present."

"He's not paying attention," Tim said, although, for once, Adam clearly was. "What is this about? What exactly happened?"

"Just what Joanne said," her mother answered. "And I'm very upset about it." She looked at Joanne disapprovingly.

"You're so ..." She searched for the word. "Insensitive," she concluded, but shook her head, still searching.

Tim smirked. "Wait. Someone posted a—" he cleared his throat and continued, "pic? Do you think it was a prank? Like one of those YouTubers who films reactions or something?"

"That's totally possible," Joanne agreed. "Poor mom!" She met her brother's eye and they simultaneously laughed, united in delight at their mother's discomfiture.

"It's just this kind of thing ..." Joanne's father began. He shook his head. A switch had flipped, Joanne could see, and she stopped smiling. Her father's eyebrows were pointed in on themselves, making him look like an angry Muppet. "These kids. These—excuse my French—fucking little shits."

"Dad," Tim said, his eyes darting to his wife.

"Sorry." Joanne's father also looked at Katrina. "Sorry," he said again. "It's just that I saw it every day at school. It's a good thing you decided to get out of the city." He pointed his fork at his daughter-in-law, who nodded slowly, her lips pushed together. "You should have come out here instead of going to Jersey, but I guess this place is going to sh–hell too. People putting dirty pictures up in the grocery store," he concluded contemptuously. He put down his fork and nodded to indicate his wife. "Really threw this one into a tailspin. Most action she's seen in years."

Joanne's mother slammed both palms down, but given the tablecloth and pad underneath it, the resultant thump was dull and unrewarding. She shook her head and fled, for the second time that day, to the kitchen.

"Mom," Joanne called, lamely, after her.

"Jesus, Dad," Tim said. "This isn't *Married, with Children.*"

"She used to be able to take a joke," their father said, shrugging. "Must be the menopause."

"Umm, I think that ship has sailed," Joanne said. "I'll go check on her."

***

Her mother would only say that she'd "had enough" and wouldn't return to the table, so Joanne started slicing up the remains of the roast and they sat at the kitchen island, eating the meat alone together.

"I've just had enough," her mother said. "The swearing and your father's jokes and everyone laughing at me."

"No one was laughing at you."

"You were," her mother said pointedly. "Both you and Timmy were. And it's not funny. I'm very upset about what happened today."

Joanne nodded. "Sorry. Maybe you should talk to someone at the store or something?"

"I really should," her mother said. "Will you come with me?"

"Sure," Joanne said, not dreaming that her mother would remain aggrieved after the holiday.

Joanne's phone chimed twice in quick succession. One text was from Tim, asking if their mother was okay and if they should clear the dishes. The second was from her father, asking "Mom ok?" accompanied by a split screen image of a horse and a smiling Alexandria Ocasio-Cortez. The caption read, "I'm Mr. Ed and I'm Special Ed."

She texted her brother, telling him to get everyone in the den and that she'd clean up, that they needed another minute.

"What's wrong with Dad?" Joanne asked. "All this AOC stuff."

Her mother shrugged. "He's always been conservative."

"This is something new."

Joanne's mother frowned and moved her head from side-to-side before saying, "He was the same way about Sarah Palin."

"But Palin really was a moron. She was the worst."

"Hmmm," her mother responded, non-committal. "She certainly wasn't for everyone."

"Plus, Dad's gotten so… nasty," Joanne continued.

Her mother's eyes filled with tears. "He's had a difficult couple of months at school."

"Did something happen?"

Joanne's mother rose to put away the roast.

Both of Joanne's parents were teachers; her mother taught elementary, and her father taught high school in Queens, that mythical land fifteen miles to the west, where the population was increasingly, according to her parents, not-white and non-English-speaking and incapable of safe driving and strange-smelling and rude.

"It's hard to be a male teacher these days," her mother explained. "There was a time when students had more respect for male teachers. But now ..." She trailed off, sealing a freezer bag of sliced beef and putting it in the fridge. She turned back to Joanne. "He's getting older, too. The kids just don't listen to him like they used to. They don't listen to anyone like they used to." She smiled sadly. "But he never should have stayed with teaching to begin with. He should have gone into administration. Teaching has become so ... feminized."

"That's not a new thing," Joanne pointed out. She was about to say more—she knew quite a bit about this, she wanted to tell her mother, and in fact she had taken an urban studies class that had looked specifically at public education in New York City, but her mother continued.

"I think he felt a bit betrayed. He thought other men would be coming aboard. But they never did," she said. "And some of the other teachers—the women—have been really mean to him."

"What are you talking about?" Joanne asked, abandoning the mini-lecture she'd been preparing in her head. "Mean to him? How?"

Joanne's mother shrugged. "You know how women are."

"No, I don't, actually," Joanne said.

"Oh, Joanne," her mother said sharply. "Not everything has to be an argument!" She turned and rinsed the platter off in the sink.

Joanne didn't respond and a moment later, she realized her mother was sobbing. Joanne stepped beside her and took the platter out of her hands.

"Oh, Mom," she said. "Are you okay? What's going on?"

"All I wanted was a nice Christmas," her mother said. "And it's started off so badly. What with that ... visual assault at the store. I just can't get over it."

A part of Joanne admired her mother's phrasing, but another part of her found the overreaction cringy and ridiculous, and these two warring responses canceled each other out, leading to silence.

She was a nice mom, overall. Maybe a little prudish, a little dramatic. A little judgmental. Racist in theory more than in practice, she had a surprisingly diverse clutch of friends, though privately she often said terrible—even heartless—things about those friends' exact ethnic groups. She was self-righteously sexist, but who wasn't, at least among her mother's cohort?

She loved crafts, and Disney, and Richard Gere, and Christmas. She was pretty basic, as moms went, which maybe wasn't a terrible thing. So, Joanne rubbed her back and let it go, resolving to try and be a little nicer the next day, to make sure her mother got the Christmas she deserved.

***

Joanne was in the darkened den when Tim came in and sat next to her on the sofa.

"What are you doing?" he asked.

"Nothing." She laid her phone face down on her thigh. "Everybody else went to bed?"

He nodded and picked up the remote.

"Wanna watch something?"

"Sure."

They sat staring dumbly at the looming television as Tim cycled through various menus.

"Gonna call Cass while you're here?" Tim asked.

"Yeah, after Christmas," Joanne said. Cass was a childhood friend who, tragically, at least according to Joanne, still lived in the area. Though Cass was a bit of a cypher—strange and tightlipped and often cold—she intrigued Joanne. And Joanne liked her. She was whip smart, for one thing. And then, Joanne had always felt a bit solicitous of her friend. Cass had been teased a lot in middle school—perhaps even more than chubby baby-Joanne—because her family was poor. Her parents were the kind of de-fanged elder hippies whose apparent anti-establishment pratices lacked bite, whose vague principles seemed cherry-picked to support their general laziness. "She says she's getting married again," Joanne added.

"Jeez," Tim said. "Maybe she should give it a rest. Marriage isn't all it's cracked up to be."

"Well, maybe it's not for everyone," Joanne said.

"Yeah," Tim agreed. "But things are good with you? You dating anyone?"

"I'm seeing a couple of different people."

"Eww."

"What?"

"Sorry I asked."

"Yeah, I'm sorry you asked too," Joanne said. "It's not, like, sordid," she added.

"Whatever," her brother said. "I guess you shouldn't rush to settle down." Tim continued scrolling through the television menus. "Should we just go to Blockbuster?"

"Ha," Joanne said. "But you know, I kind of miss Blockbuster. It gave a shape to things. Especially at the holidays."

"Yeah," Tim agreed. He laughed a little through his nose, a prefatory snort to indicate that he thought his next comment would be amusing. "Katrina and I have never had a Blockbuster fight. You know, the fight where you both say you don't care what you watch but you really do and then you take it personally when whoever you're with chooses something they should know you'll hate? Revealing how little they know you? Or how little they care? And then you pick something, and they get pissed and then you storm out without anything at all?"

"I'm sure you and Katrina find other things to fight about."

"You got that right. Have you seen this yet?" He stopped on the new James Bond.

"Nope," Joanne said. "Let's watch it."

"Nah," Tim said. He continued scanning. "So, what the hell was that all about at dinner?"

"Which part?"

"The Mom-and-Dad-are-out-of-their-minds part."

Joanne shrugged. "Mom and Dad were raised in really repressive families and frankly it's not surprising that Mom has never been comfortable with sexuality or with herself as a sexual being. Seeing that dick pic sort of triggered—"

"Oh my God," Tim interrupted. "Stop. What is wrong with you?"

Joanne, truly unsure of what he meant, asked, "What do you mean?"

"Okay, Dr. Freud. We don't need to talk about Mom's 'sexuality.'"

"Dad did."

"And it was gross then too."

"I mean, you brought it up," Joanne said.

"Um, no I didn't." He shuddered. "You're so ..."

"What?" Joanne said, rolling her eyes.

"I don't know. You're so weird." Pulling his most well-worn weapon from an ancient arsenal, he added, "Maybe you were adopted after all."

"Don't get sentimental on me," Joanne said. "And I'm not weird. Maybe you guys are the weird ones."

"I suppose that's possible," Tim said. "But you ... you're like an alien from another planet, still familiarizing yourself with our ways. You're an X-File."

"I really enjoy spending time with you too, Timmy," Joanne said.

"I'm not trying to be an asshole. I almost respect it. Like you really, honestly don't care what other people think. How did that happen?"

"I do care," Joanne said. "A lot. So much, actually, that this conversation is becoming a bit painful to me."

"I'm sorry," her brother said. "I'm not trying to hurt your feelings. You're fine. I didn't mean it."

"God, that just makes it worse."

"Try and take it as a compliment."

Joanne rolled her eyes in the dim light. "Whatever, Tim."

"So what do you think really happened at Fresh Country Farms?" Tim asked.

Joanne was angry and hurt, and no longer interested in talking to her brother. She picked up her phone. "Who knows."

"Well, I'm never shopping there again."

"They have really nice breads, though," Joanne said.

"You still eat carbs?" Tim said. "Yeah, I guess, of course you do."

***

After presents and then the post-unwrapping attempts to disguise disappointment and then pancakes and the post-pancake vocalizations of self-loathing, Joanne's mother asked her if she was ready to go to Fresh Country Farms.

"Now?" Joanne said.

"Yes. I want to get it over with."

"But it's Christmas," Joanne said.

"They're open," her mother returned.

"Thank the Jews," her father remarked.

"But, Mom," Joanne tried. "Really? Now?"

She was still in her pajamas. They had *The March of the Wooden Soldiers* on the TV, ostensibly for Adam, who had nodded absently when they'd proposed the colorized black-and-white movie but who now made no pretense of watching.

"Well, I guess it would be nice to take a walk," Joanne said finally. It was another mild day.

"We should drive," her mother responded. "In case we have to make a quick getaway."

"Why would we have to make a quick getaway?"

"You never know," her mother answered darkly.

"We're walking," Joanne said, heaving herself—that's how she imagined that they saw her, as though she had to heave her huge, fat, obese body—off the couch.

"Are you bringing a purse?" her mother, looming in the doorway, asked.

"A purse? No," Joanne said. She cut a smirk at Timmy, but he was looking at his phone.

"Well, put this in your pocket," her mother instructed, handing her a small pink canister: the pepper spray Joanne had received in her stocking that morning.

"Mom," Joanne groaned.

"Just do it," her mother said, turning away.

***

They walked together down the eerily still, sidewalkless streets of their suburban town. Everyone, Joanne imagined, was inside, enjoying their new electronics and jewelry and niche-interest coffee table books. Her phone chimed and then, a moment later, her mother's did too.

It was a group text from her father to all of them: Joanne, Tim, Katrina, and Joanne's mom. It read, *don't let your mother get herself arrested.* And then, in keeping with his apparent compulsion, he texted a gif of AOC in a photoshopped tee-shirt that read, "MABA: Make Alexandria Bartend Again."

"Your father?" Joanne's mother asked.

"Yeah," she answered glumly.

"He does have a problem," Joanne's mother said.

"I agree."

"Not that. What we were talking about last night. He's been rubber-roomed."

"What?"

"He's not in the high school anymore. He has to go to the central office every day. They put him in the rubber room."

"Holy shit, Mom. What happened?"

"Please watch your language, Joanne. It was…a group of…girls. Some of the girls complained about him."

"About what?"

"Some of the things he said in class."

"Like, inappropriate things?"

Dirty Suburbia

Her eyes on the ground ahead, her mother nodded solemnly.

"What kinds of inappropriate things?"

Her mother waved a hand in the air, as though the specifics were unimportant. "He was joking around. You know how he is."

"What exactly did he say?"

"He'll retire at the end of this year. And he'll keep his pension. The union can at least do that for him."

"Jesus Christ. What did he say, Mom?"

Joanne's mother looked at her sharply, her face deeply creased. "It's not his fault. And please don't tell him I told you. He's already so upset. It's an overreaction—a witch hunt, even. Everyone's all in a lather over this 'Me Too' nonsense. Not that that some of those men don't deserve it. But other people get caught up. And you know how teenagers are." She paused. "Please don't tell Timmy. He'd be so upset."

"I don't even know what to say," Joanne said.

They'd arrived at Fresh Country Farms.

"Let's not talk any more about it," her mother said. "Let's just go ahead and handle this."

***

Joanne, stunned, followed her mother through the doors that gently hummed and swooshed open into the nearly-empty store, instrumental Christmas music issuing from hidden speakers. Only one checkout lane was open. The cashier glanced up at them and then returned to looking for split ends in her hair.

Her mother pointed to the TV, "Let's watch first," she said.

They stood, gazing up at the garlanded screen, which read "Happy Holidays" before transitioning to a picture of some incredibly unappetizing chicken breasts, half-price until 12/27.

The video cycled through several more unflattering photos of food. This screen seemed, to Joanne, to be the opposite of advertising. What would that be? Discouragement? Repulsion?

"Do you need something?" the cashier called suspiciously.

Joanne tried to perk up, to keep her face open and friendly, and took a step closer to the checkout. "Actually, is there a manager around?"

The cashier scowled in reply and picked up a phone. She said something in Spanish, a language Joanne was ostensibly studying as part of her graduate degree but which continued to fundamentally elude her..

Waiting, Joanne continued to watch the awful screen. "I just can't get over that thing about Dad," she said out of the side of her mouth.

"Please, don't bring it up again," her mother whispered back. "I shouldn't have told you."

A man approached wearing a blue vest and a Santa hat. He was Joanne's age, or maybe a little older, olive-skinned and smiling, a perfect dimple on either side of his face.

"Happy holidays!" he said. "Can I help you ladies with something?"

Joanne looked at her mother, waiting for her to respond, and when she didn't, Joanne cleared her throat. "My mom was here yesterday," she began. "And when she was waiting on line, she saw something upsetting." She pointed up to the TV. The manager, whose name tag read Jonhnny—spelled just like that, with that extra, unusual "n"—continued to smile at them, but he tilted his head quizzically, encouraging Joanne to go on. He exuded an upbeat friendliness. Joanne had expected to find a manager embittered to be working on Christmas. Jonhnny's good humor made this more difficult, she thought.

"It was ... perverse," Joanne said at last. "It was a penis. On the screen."

Jonhnny stopped smiling. "What?" he asked.

"Yeah," Joanne said, exhaling and nodding, a tiny, awkward smile on her lips. "Yeah."

"Are you sure it wasn't just, like, a zucchini or something?" Jonhnny asked her mother.

"That's what I said!" Joanne exclaimed.

"I know the difference between a penis and a zucchini!" Joanne's mother snapped, much too loud, and Joanne heard a muffled cackle from behind the register.

Jonhnny touched Joanne's elbow and guided them away from the checkout and toward the salad dressings.

"I am so sorry, Mrs ...?"

"Fitzgerald," her mother said.

"I have no idea how something like that could have happened. It's so ... I just don't know how that could have gotten up there."

"Maybe an employee was playing a prank or something? Or is was hacked?" Joanne offered.

Jonhnny's eyes widened and he shook his head, suggesting she was blowing his mind. He said, "I really have no idea. We've never had a situation like this before."

"A child could have seen it," Joanne's mother said. "It's totally inappropriate. I thought this was a family store!"

"It is, absolutely. It's ... unconscionable," Jonhnny said. "I really don't know what to say. Look, let me get your information, and I'll investigate and let you know once I get to the bottom of this."

"I could sue," Joanne's mother continued, as though she hadn't heard him. "My daughter is a lawyer."

"I'm not a lawyer," Joanne said, twisting up her face.

"Not you," her mother said. "Katrina. My daughter-in-law," she added, annoyed.

"Oh," Joanne said, blinking. "Look," she said, turning to Jonhnny. "I'm sure it won't come to that."

"I can't tell you how sorry I am that this happened to you, Mrs. Fitzgerald," Jonhnny said. "Let me get your phone number and I'll definitely be in touch once I have more information."

Jonhnny took a notebook out of his back pocket and waited, pencil poised.

"I'm Joanne," Joanne said. "You can call me." She took a step closer to him and watched as he wrote "Jo-Anne," underlined it, and then took down her phone number. He wrote very carefully and, when he was done, he looked up at her, the white pompom on his Santa hat bobbing, and smiled.

"Mom," Joanne said. "Why don't you go ahead outside and get some fresh air? I'll be right behind you."

Her mother glowered, and it occurred to Joanne she was jealously guarding her self-righteous rage, clutching it to herself like a cherished treasure.

"Just a minute, Mom. I promise I'll be right out."

Jonhnny and Joanne watched as Joanne's mother, after a final angry glance at the television, made her way to the door.

"I don't know what to say. I'm so sorry about this," Jonhnny said.

He really did seem sorry, and Joanne felt compelled to comfort him in turn. "No, I'm sorry. I mean, I believe her and everything, but apparently she's been under a lot of stress. Maybe she hallucinated it?"

Jonhnny widened his eyes. "Do you think that's possible?" He shook his head, and pompom flying, concluded no, it was not. "I think it's more likely that someone thought they would pull a prank. People do crazy stuff these days." She noticed that his eyes darted to the cash registers. The woman there probably didn't have a penis on hand, so to speak, but she might have access to someone else's.

"Even so, she's kind of overreacting," Joanne said. "It's almost funny? So, I'm sorry. It probably sucks to have to work on Christmas anyway and then to have people showing up and complaining…"

"No, no," he said. "And it's not so bad. We close early. And this way I get New Year's off."

"Well, that's good," Joanne said.

"You live around here?"

"My parents do. I live in the city."

He nodded. "Cool. I live in Queens. But I actually have plans in Manhattan on New Year's. We should meet up."

Joanne met Jonhnny's eye. She smiled and he smiled too and his dimples, those tiny revelations, reappeared. "Oh," she said. "Sure. That could work."

"I've got your number," he said, patting the pad that he had returned to his back pocket. "I'll text you so you'll have mine."

"Yeah," she said. She liked how un-self-consciously he wore that Santa hat. "Just, um, no dick pics, okay?"

Jonhnny's face moved quickly from shock to delight and he threw his head back and hooted with laughter.

They were both still smiling as he walked her to the door, past the cashier, who watched them with a contempt so profound it was almost comical. But Joanne flashed a smile at her anyway, and she could have sworn the cashier almost smiled back.

***

"I wish you hadn't contradicted me in front of that man," Joanne's mother said as soon as the doors sucked closed behind her. "Suggesting that I was lying about my daughter being a lawyer."

"Mom, I didn't know what you were talking about. Plus, Katrina hasn't practiced law in years."

"She could write a letter."

"She would never do that."

"She might if I asked her. But that's not the point. You shouldn't have contradicted me."

"Okay, sorry." Joanne sighed. "But the manager seemed nice. I really think he'll follow up."

"It could have been his," her mother said, frowning. "For all we know it could have been his."

Joanne considered that it would have been fun to make a joke then, to ask just how enormous the penis had been, but she resisted. "He didn't seem like that type of person to me," she said instead.

Her mother raised her eyebrows to suggest otherwise.

"There is something else I wanted to talk to you about, Joanne," her mother said. "Something Daddy wanted me to talk to you about."

Joanne felt the smile that had been lurking behind her eyes fading from her face. "What's up?"

"It's your weight, honey. We're just all so worried about you. You know, you have such a pretty face—"

Joanne's cheeks flushed, a wave of outrage at the banality of her mother's words. She tried to load her words with warning: "Stop."

Her mother was undeterred. "Katrina has a friend in the city who's a nutritionist..."

"Wait, you talked to Katrina about this? When did you 'all' get together and talk about me behind my back?"

"No one was talking behind your back," her mother said dismissively. "We were waiting for you to come down this morning and Daddy mentioned it and... we all just want you to be healthy."

"The real question is, what does Adam think?"

Joanne's mother paused. "Well, I don't know that Addie thinks anything. He was on the iPad."

"I was kidding, mom. For god's sake, I really don't—"

"Honey, we just want you to be happy. How are you ever going to meet anyone unless you lose weight?"

"I'm doing just fine in that department, actually," Joanne snapped. "As a matter of fact, Jonhnny just asked me out."

"Who?"

"The guy. The manager at Fresh Country Farms."

Her mother stopped walking and Joanne did too. "Well, mystery solved. It must have been his..." She waved a hand in the air before moving along. "On the screen."

"What?" Joanne didn't continue walking, so her mother had to turn back. She looked impatient.

"Don't be naïve, Joanne. I don't want to have to spell it out for you. They have a term for those kind of deviants. 'Chubby chasers,'" her mother said, pursing her lips.

Joanne almost, but did not, laugh. "What is wrong with you? Why would you say that?"

Her mother stepped in close. "You're making a scene. Please, Joanne."

"That was such a fucked-up thing to say," Joanne growled.

"Don't you use that language with me," her mother said. "I'm just trying to be honest with you. You're deluding yourself," her mother insisted.

"Me? You are the one hallucinating cocks!" Joanne bellowed in her mother's face. Then she marched forward angrily, past all the neat houses shut up tight in the weak December sun, leaving her shocked mother to walk home alone.

***

did they have you look at a line up? her father wrote in the group text.

Her brother replied with a face that was laughing so hard it was crying.

Joanne put her phone back in her pocket and let herself into the house. She'd planned to flee directly to her room, or rather, the smaller bedroom that she had to occupy until Tim's family left, but her father, laying in wait, blocked the staircase.

"We talked to a manager," Joanne told him impatiently. She gestured for her father to move. With his canny nose for conflict, he narrowed his eyes and stayed put.

"What exactly did he tell you?" he asked. "Where's your mother?"

"She's right behind me."

"Is she okay?"

"I'm fine," her mother answered, pulling the door shut. "But the pervert manager hit on Joanne."

Without missing a beat, Joanne's father said, "I suppose dating the owner of a supermarket would be right up your alley, Joanne. But you might put him out of business."

Joanne blinked. "What is wrong with you," she said. She turned and marched toward the kitchen.

"Joanne!" her mother shouted after her. Behind her, she heard her mother chiding her father: "Not nice."

Katrina and Adam sat hunched like buzzards at the kitchen island, looking at their devices. Joanne's sister-in-law straightened up, eyes wide and startled, as usual. "Is everything okay?" she asked.

Several phones chimed. When Joanne looked at hers, she saw an image of a fat child who had been on a reality TV series. The image was accompanied by some sort of sassy and ostensibly body-positive caption. It was, Joanne considered, her father's version of an apology. Putting the phone in her back pocket, she felt an unfamiliar lump, like a lipstick. It was the mace. She put the phone in her other pocket and moved toward the sliding doors that led to the deck.

"And you suck too, Katrina," Joanne said. She tried to yank open the door, but her parents had installed an elaborate lock. She felt breathless and panicky. She had to get out. "I'm sorry," she said, switching switches and pushing and pulling. "I didn't mean that. But I don't want to talk to your nutritionist friend."

Katrina rose and, with a flash of her tiny, glittering fingers, unhinged the newly-installed metal rod between the sliding doors. "I know," she said. "I didn't really want to have anything to do with that conversation." She slid open the door. "Here you go."

"Thanks, Katrina," Joanne said. "I just need a fucking minute."

Her phone pinged again and, unable to help herself, Joanne retrieved it. It was a text from Tim this time, again sent to the whole family. When she opened it, she saw a photo of an erect penis, clutched, as her mother would say, by a hand. Behind the penis, Joanne could clearly see the Christmas quilt her mother had labored over the previous year.

"What the fuck?" Joanne said. She stepped back into the kitchen to see Katrina, who had returned to the island, and was again hunched over her phone.

"Um, I guess he didn't mean to send that to the group text?" Joanne said, incredulous. In another room, her mother yelped. For her part, Joanne let out a nervous laugh. But then Katrina looked up, her face at once pinched and drawn, and Joanne frowned and cleared her throat. There was a thumping from the upstairs, like someone falling off a bed or knocking over a chair.

"Adam, go to the den," Katrina said, her mouth barely moving.

Adam didn't move. "What happened?" he asked. "What's on the phone?"

They heard the sound of footsteps as Tim flew down the stairs, and then murmured voices as his parents tried to intercept him. A moment later, Tim was barreling into the kitchen.

"I'm so sorry you guys," he said. His parents were on his heels, almost crashing into him when he stopped abruptly. "That was not for everyone. That was just for Katrina," he said, just to Katrina.

Katrina frowned and shook her head almost imperceptibly. "Let me see your phone," she said, holding out her hand, palm up.

They watched, Joanne and her mom and her dad, as Katrina and Tim gazed at each other. "Like a joke," Tim said, a slight whine in his voice. "About what happened to my mom at the grocery store."

Katrina left her hand in the air. She appeared impassive. Tim inhaled. He too shook his head. "It's not what you think," he said. "You have to let me explain."

Katrina lowered her hand and stood. "No, I don't." She let herself out onto the deck.

"What is happening?" Joanne's mother asked Tim. "Timmy, how did that picture ...? Who ...? What happened?"

"Don't be so naïve, Marcy," Joanne's father snapped.

Joanne followed Katrina out onto the deck.

"Are you okay?" Joanne asked her sister-in-law.

Before Katrina could answer, though, there they were again, her parents and Tim and Adam, yanking open the sliding door, tumbling out behind them.

"How about everyone goes back inside? I need to talk to my wife in private," Tim barked.

"This is your fault," Joanne's father said to Joanne.

"My fault?" Joanne asked, disbelieving. "My fault? Timmy is the one sending dick pics!" She turned to her mother. "Maybe he was the one who posted his penis at Fresh Country Farms."

Her mother gasped.

"How dare you," her father said. "You are disgusting."

"I'm disgusting? I'm disgusting? What did you say to those girls, Dad? Why are you rubber-roomed?" Joanne spat back.

"Oh, Joanne," Joanne's mother gasped. She cast her eyes to the ground, disappointed, betrayed.

"What are you talking about now?" Tim asked, his eyes darting from his mother to his father to his sister.

"Dad, like, sexually harassed some girls," Joanne said to her brother. "Maybe the tendency is genetic?"

"That's not what happened," her father snarled. "How dare you. Who do you think you are?" He looked at her mother. "We've created a monster, Marcy."

And suddenly she felt like a monster, but the big, weak, cowering kind, and she backed further away from them, this familial mob gathered in a semi-circle around her. All they lacked were pitchforks.

"Come inside," Tim said to Katrina, a frantic, beseeching edge in his voice. "We don't need to be doing this out in the backyard." He cut a glance at the neighbor's house. "And put that away," he hissed at his son, who seemed to be recording the exchange on his iPad.

Joanne caught Katrina's eye. "Let's go," she whimpered. "Let's just leave."

"You're not leaving with my wife," Tim said.

Joanne only spoke to Katrina. "Let's go. Right? We'll take your car? We should just get out of here."

"Hey," her father said, his face red, his lips almost comically thin. "That's enough out of you." He took a step closer and poked at the air in front of her face. She saw the burst veins around his nose, his runny eyes. His breath was warm and, she thought, smelled of peanut butter. "You've caused enough problems already. You need to learn shut your fat mouth."

Joanne almost laughed. But she did as he said; she shut her big fat mouth.

She was too much, she knew then. She was simply too much for them.

She'd loved them once, and they'd loved her. A series of images flickered through her mind, memories of her father in a Santa suit, of her father making her laugh with his hilarious jokes at others' expenses, of her father, getting into a shoving match with another man over a call at one of her little league games.

She thought of her mother, too, the first person she called if she felt even slightly less than robustly healthy, the only person who ever asked what happened when she wore a band-aid, her gentle, often-sweet, mom.

She loved them, but she didn't really feel like they loved her back that much anymore. It hurt, but it was okay. She knew she was not for everyone.

She would have liked to have left then, but her father's body was blocking her escape, and he persisted in jabbing his stubby finger in her face as he continued to berate her, his finger so close she had to flinch, to wonder if he would poke her right over the railing of the deck.

Her hands moved to her backside. She slid the pepper spray out of her pocket and held the canister in front of his face. His rich, brownie-batter eyes bulged momentarily and Joanne found it the easiest thing in the world, to push aside the safety and press down with her thumb. A stringy white substance like spit—or something else—streamed into her father's angry, ugly face. Joanne cringed and dropped her hand.

She heard her mother screaming. Her father, also bellowing, fell to his knees on the hardwood deck, his hands over his eyes.

"Joanne!" her mother wailed. She rushed to her husband's side and then began to push Joanne. Her mother was using both hands and seemed to be exerting herself, but the shove was so ineffectual it almost seemed playful. Her face, though, was a picture of pain. "Leave," she panted. "You. Go."

Katrina stepped between them then. "Yes," she said to Joanne. "Let's go."

***

The car loaded with whatever belongings they could grab in a mad dash, as though they were starring in an episode of *Supermaket Sweep* crossed with a Lifetime movie about family dysfunction, Joanne and Katrina drove down the street that Joanne and her mother had walked just an hour before, although it was twilight now and people's Christmas decorations—the colorful lights and Santa inflatables and glowing plastic figures—were shining like early evening stars. She thought that the neighborhood presented like the towns in train sets, snug houses with glowing windows and no one inside. Joanne tried to slow her breathing.

They passed the strip mall where the Blockbuster used to be and then the darkened Fresh Country Farms.

Joanne thought of her friend Cass and was sorry she wouldn't see her. Maybe Cass could come to the city, though. It might do her some good to escape this sordid suburb, even if only for an evening.

"Do you really think your mom saw a dick?" Katrina asked softly.

Just at that moment a text appeared from an unknown number; when Joanne opened it, she saw the image of a white man, smiling with his lips closed. The text underneath read,

hi its jonhnny. Sry again about what happened but glad I met u. Merry xmas and lets hang on new years!

Joanne exhaled loudly. "Oh my god," she said. "That's really funny."

"What?" Katriina asked. "What is?"

"It's another dick pic," Joanne said, flashing the image of former Vice President Cheney at her sister-in-law. "From the manager of the grocery store."

Katrina paused and then agreed: "That is funny."

They rode along in silence.

"Thanks for getting me out of there," Joanne said at last.

"Yeah, well, thanks for getting *me* out of there."

"What the fuck, right?"

Katrina shook her head, and then she started to breathe hard through her nose. Joanne felt a giggle bubble up in her chest, and then their hilarity broke like a wave, an exquisite and ongoing relief, and they traveled that way together, hooting and cackling and crying, screaming and howling down the dim and quiet Christmas streets.

REVENGE OF THE NERDS

Because my mom is a psycho-bitch, my grandparents had to take her to court in order to be able to see me. And because my father is, legit, I am not exaggerating, a convicted rapist *who also still has parental rights,* my mother has to stay in Wisconsin so that if he ever chooses to exercise his privileges he may do so.

Obviously, it's all totally fucked.

Especially since every July my mother has to drive me to Fort Lee, New Jersey, where her sister meets us at a diner or a McDonald's so that I can be transported (at no extra cost to my mother), over several bridges to Queens, to the house where my aunt and grandparents live. After two weeks, my aunt drives me all the way back to Wisconsin. She doesn't mind paying all those tolls, I guess.

This year, we meet at a Starbucks, which is an upgrade. The glass door makes a sucking sound when my mother pulls it open, and we are blasted with clean, cool air. It feels good after getting out of the sticky car, walking through the steamy parking lot, the sun so bright that I could only manage to squint one eye open.

When my aunt sees us, she puts down her phone and stands up. I imagine how we must look to her: me, sweaty, fatter, more pissed-off, and my mom, my once-beautiful mom, with her dirty hair and her slouching shoulders and her tits dangling like overfull water balloons.

My aunt isn't such hot shit either. She looks like my mom, but rounder, healthier, less-insane.

My aunt and my mom do some sort of weird almost-hug and then my aunt rubs my shoulder. Her hand is cold. She must have been waiting a long time. "Do you guys want to get a coffee or something?" my aunt asks. "Before you get back on the road?"

"Sure," my mom says. "You buying?"

She is so cheap. Why is she so cheap?

My aunt ignores her and smiles tightly at me. "What do you want, Dig?"

"I'll have a low-fat white chocolate mocha Frappuccino," I say.

"I don't know if I'll be able to remember that," my aunt replies while my mother rolls her eyes. "Come with me to order." I follow her to the counter. "I like your new glasses," my aunt says brightly, as we wait in the line.

"Thanks," I say. I wanted to get the black, chunky frames everyone started wearing last fall, at the beginning of freshman year. But instead of cute and ironic, my glasses, from Walmart, are ugly and dumb. I look like a senior citizen. God, my life is so stupid.

Dirty Suburbia

"My mother calls me '*Revenge of the Nerds*,'" I tell my aunt. "I don't even know what that means."

She laughs through her nose. "It's a gross movie from the eighties," she says. "But your glasses are cool."

We order our drinks, and my aunt goes back to the table and gets herself up-to-date on all of my mother's complaints while I wait at the counter. I wonder if my mother is saying anything about me. Although I'd like to, I can't hear them over the Starbucks indie rock and chatter. I feel like a ghost who can't filter out the conversations all around me, who can't focus in on the people I actually want to listen to.

"One tall coffee and one Grande low-fat white chocolate mocha Frappuccino for Dignity?" the coffee guy calls into my face. "Cute name," he adds as I take the drinks.

When I sit back down, my mother nods at my Frappuccino and says, "That's supposed to be a coffee?" as though people haven't been making that remark about fancy coffee drinks since the dawn of time.

I shake my head, disgusted with her lack of originality.

"Put your headphones on," my mother commands. "I want to talk to your aunt."

I get on the Starbucks WiFi and pretend to watch my show, but really, I listen.

Not that it's anything interesting. They cycle through the same three topics they always do: how much my mother hates my grandparents, how hard my mother's life is, how much my father sucks. It's like when people are driving cars in old movies, how the same background comes around again and again. And whatever, we haven't heard from my father recently. The last time I even saw him was three years ago, right after he got out of prison for kidnapping and raping his ex-girlfriend.

My mother told me that the fact that it was his ex-girlfriend made it not so bad. What she actually said was: "Your dad is more of a JV rapist. You know? It's not like he's one of those guys who jumps out of the bushes." She sighed. "He's not even a varsity rapist."

I didn't bother to point out that he did, in fact, quite literally jump out of the bushes in front of his ex-girlfriend's apartment complex. And he was holding an axe. An axe! What the fuck?

And the worst part of the whole thing is that this wasn't even the first time he had done this. It was the second time.

Same woman, both times. No axe the first time, though. It was really the axe that got him locked up in the end, it seemed.

***

My mother, in an inexplicable mercy, never made me visit my father in prison. But when he got out, my mother announced, after some sort of extended negotiation with a social worker, that we would be meeting up with him at—where else?—a McDonald's.

Because my father was living in a halfway house in Illinois and because my mom sure hates paying a toll, this particular McDonald's was in the Belvidere Oasis: one of those rest stops in a bridge over the highway, which of course could work as some sort of metaphor. I don't know.

What I do know is that I was wearing my brand-new powder blue pleather jacket on the dark October afternoon that we went to the Belvidere Oasis. I thought I looked so fucking cool in that stupid jacket. And, though I cringe to recall this, and although the reason remains a mystery to me, I wanted my stupid father to think that I was cool. Or something. And so even though I began to sweat immediately after walking into the dim, warm, French-fry smelling Belvidere Oasis, I refused to take the jacket off.

"Take off your jacket," I remember my mother demanding. "You're gonna overheat."

"I'm fine," I hissed back.

We spotted my father, sitting alone at a table. His stringy hair matched my mother's.

***

Now, I shiver a little bit in the Starbucks. They've got the air turned up too high.

My phone vibrates with a text from David.

u here?

In his pictures, David looks like Pete Davidson, the cute skinny guy from *Saturday Night Live*, who dates celebrities and has a famously big dick. From the pictures David sent me, I think he probably does too. I guess I'll find out for sure soon enough.

I look up to see if my mother is trying to read my texts, but I see she is busy crying, rubbing viciously at her red eyes.

My aunt and grandparents say that my mother is the way she is because she is the baby of the family. I say she is the way she is because she's a fucking psycho. But what do I know? I'm an only child. At least that's what I've been told.

I take my headphones off. "It's just two weeks, Kiera," my aunt is telling my mother. "Try to enjoy it. Try to do things for yourself."

My mother looks at me and hides her face in her hands. "I'm sorry," she says. She peeks out and gives me a pathetic little smile. "I'm just gonna miss you, Dignity."

I get up and put my arms around her and sit on her lap. This makes her laugh. I kiss her on her smelly head.

"I'm going to miss you too," I say.

She holds me tightly around the waist and sobs into my neck. "My baby," she says, and I feel like crying too, but only for a minute.

***

In the car, my aunt is talking about some cousin who finished high school in three years and blah blah blah. I text David back, *yea*

He texts, *c u 2nite?*

I lay my phone face down on my knee.

I hate when he uses abbreviations like "2nite." I feel like he's just doing it to seem younger. It makes me feel like he's a pedophile or something. I mean, we did meet online, but it's not that weird for adults to game, and it's not like he was on there looking for a girlfriend. Or at least that's what he says.

The car is quiet, and I wonder how long ago my aunt stopped talking. I look out the window at the skyline. It was in front of us; now it's beside us. We will continue to glide right past it.

How do you know Im not a cop? I text David, just to be a jerk.

He doesn't respond right away. Then he writes, *wtf?*

lollolololol, I write.

He sends back a gif of a sexy female cop. I lay my phone face down again.

***

In Queens, after dinner, I sit on the loveseat behind my grandparents and aunt, who are each installed in their designated recliners in the TV room. David texts to tell me to take the subway and meet him in a place called "Flushing" which obviously sounds super-fucking romantic. I don't want to tell him that I've never actually taken the subway by myself before. I don't even know how you pay to get on it. My aunt or grandmother always sort of shepherds me around when we go anywhere. I guess I could Google it. But I also think he should just pick me up. I've come all this way and now he's being cheap or something.

I write: *whatever im tired from the car. ill text you tmw*
He writes: *wtf*

I don't text back.

He keeps them coming.

what's going on? I thought you wanted to see me?

im serious I just cant wait any longer

I have champagne for us

u still there/? is it cause i want u to meet me? it would just be faster if u came halfway. I'm coming from li but no prob if you want me to come get you in rego park i will. i just need to c u im dying to c u

I have a ping of pleasure at the obvious desperation.

I look up from my phone. The room is narrow and crowded with chairs and bulky furniture from dead relatives' houses, so when I say, "I think I'm gonna go out tonight," my grandparents and aunt all have to turn around from the television and crane their necks to see me sitting behind them.

"What?" my aunt asks, alarmed. "Where?"

"A friend of mine is visiting New York, staying at the beach. Out on Long Island. Her parents will pick me up. I'll sleep over and they'll bring me back tomorrow."

"But you just got here," my grandmother says.

"She's from Wisconsin?" my aunt asks. "Who is this person?"

"My friend Ariel," I say. "Don't worry. I'll be back tomorrow."

My grandmother looks at my grandfather and my grandfather looks at my aunt. She's the spokesperson. She never had any kids, but they act like she's the expert. Maybe they figure they didn't do such a hot job themselves, so they should just leave everything to her.

"It's not a big deal," I say.

They all look around at each other again.

"We could take you to the beach," my grandfather croaks pathetically. My grandmother nods.

They don't want to go to the beach. Now that dinner is over, they want me to have a bowl of pistachio ice cream while we watch *Jeopardy!* and *Wheel of Fortune* and some sort of true crime news show, maybe about a troubled teenager from Wisconsin who meets a guy online who lures her out to Long Island. After she is raped and dismembered, my grandmother will make some devastatingly callous remark about how people get what they deserve, and I will have a fleeting but acute understanding of how my mother came to be the way she is.

I feel a tinge of longing for this scene. Staying home with them is fine. Yes, it is boring, but I am the guest of honor. I know they like to have me here. I mean, they took my mother to court over it. Maybe I should just stay put, at least on this first night.

I am about to text David to say forget it when my aunt raises a palm to my grandfather. "She's getting older. She doesn't want to just sit around." She nods at me and says, "I think that would be okay."

"Great," I say, putting my phone down and looking at their worried, moon-like faces. "Cool."

***

Waiting for David on Queens Boulevard—the road my grandparents call the "Boulevard of Death" because so many pedestrians get hit by cars trying to cross it—I look inside my backpack to check on my stupid contraption. I wrapped a kitchen knife in a dish towel and then secured it with masking tape. It's just in case or whatever. I'm not planning to murder David.

I suppose my stupid father thought he was bringing his axe along just in case too. But if anyone is being kidnapped and raped here, it's me, not David. And I'm not going to be kidnapped and raped. David is actually my boyfriend.

Whatever, I know how it seems, him being older than me. But honestly, I am probably the more mature one in the relationship. We agree that that's the main reason I have such a hard time with people my own age. Sure, it doesn't help that I have to buy my clothes at either Walmart or Savers and that everyone in my town knows that my father is a convicted rapist. But all that aside, the idiots at my school are legitimately the worst. All the girls think they are going to be famous for doing makeup tutorials on YouTube and all the guys are just perfecting their date-rape techniques for college. Once, I was walking behind these two bros and one of them said, "Well, Morgan will only let me do it in her butt because she's saving herself for marriage." I texted that to David verbatim. I wrote, *That, right there, might be why I don't have any friends my own age.*

A black Corolla pulls up in front of me. David dips his head down so I can see his face from where I stand, so I know it is him and not a stranger. I zip up my backpack and get in.

He leans over and kisses me right away. He is chewing gum and his breath is minty.

Kissing gives me a minute to recover myself because I can't help but be just a little bit shocked. David definitely looks different than I expected. Even though I had seen a video and all that, he is still a surprise to me. He had said he was twenty-six.

"Dignity," he moans into my lips. He stops kissing me and sits back up but keeps one hand on my shoulder as we pull into traffic.

When we stop at a light, he slides his hand up and down my arm and smiles at me. He does look a little like Pete Davidson. He is thin and he has lots of earrings and even sitting down I can tell he is tall. But in-person he's almost too tall, and he has to sort of hunch over the steering wheel. And he has wrinkles around his eyes.

"We're finally together," he says.

"Yeah!" I say. I don't want him to see that I'm disappointed or to hurt his feelings. We had Facetimed or whatever. So it's not like he was lying. Although he definitely isn't twenty-six.

He kisses me again. I kiss him back, vigorously, convincingly.

A car honks and he starts driving again.

I look out the window. Because of the one-way streets, we are going to go back past my grandparent's block. For a flicker of a moment I imagine telling him to pull over, to let me out. It's like those final seconds on the roller coaster when the attendant comes around to make sure your restraint is working and you want to say, wait, let me off, but you don't because that would be so fucking embarrassing.

He tells me he is taking me to a "cool, vintage motel right near the beach." He explains that it's not the most luxurious, but its proximity to the beach makes it worth it. He's about to say more when my phone starts buzzing and I look down. My mother is texting.

what the fuck dignity where are you going who is ariana

I text back, *its fine. you dont know her*

I didn't just drive 16 hours so u could hang out with some girl from wisco get ur ass back to your grandparents

i cant, I write back. *her parents already drove all the way to queens to pick me up*

My phone starts to ring. I silence it.

"Who's that?" David asks.

"My mother," I say. "It's nothing."

"The psycho-bitch?"

"Yeah," I say. I pretend to laugh. I shake my head. "She's probably just lonely without me."

He chuckles. "She needs to give it a rest," he says. "She gets you all the time. It's my turn. Right, babe?"

The traffic has thinned out and he drives with one hand on my knee. He keeps saying things like, "I just can't believe you're really here," like I'm a celebrity or a ghost or something.

I put my hand on top of his. His fingers are long and warm. I bring his hand to my mouth and I kiss each of his fingers. He leans his head back against the headrest and groans, like I'm giving him a blow job or something. He pushes his fingers into my mouth and I suck on them—they're salty, but clean—and I'm afraid he's literally going to come in his pants, he's making such a fuss. After a while it gets kind of gross and I don't want to do it anymore, but I'm not sure how to stop either. Finally, I kiss his palm and then place his hand down on his thigh. I lean across and kiss his face. He turns his head to kiss me on the mouth and we do that for a second and then I sink back into my seat.

He puts one hand on his dick, which I can see is pressing hard against his jeans. "You are so fucking hot," he says.

We are suddenly not in the city anymore and the trees on either side of the expressway are dense and lushly green. It's not like Wisconsin, where you can see for miles and miles in every direction, the fields empty except for the skeleton-like sprinklers sprawling across flat farmland.

"Dignity," he exhales. He adjusts in his seat and clutches the steering wheel with both hands. "Your name is so perfect for you."

"My mother says she named me Dignity so I could never become a stripper," I tell him, rolling my eyes.

"Don't strippers usually change their names anyway?" he asks.

"I guess," I say. "I mean, I think she was joking."

"Psycho," he concludes, his eyes on the road.

I want to correct him. My mom is a psycho but for other reasons. She'd had been joking, and she even went on to say that she knew plenty of "sex workers," who had "great dignity." She was trying to make a larger point, about how I should expect to be treated or something. I open my mouth to begin saying this, to, like, correct the record, but he makes a hard right and we pull into the motel parking lot. The place is a one-story, weather-beaten dump. It looks like a motel in a movie about a serial killer who preys on down-on-their-luck women in central Florida.

"I know it's not super-fancy," he assures me. "But it's so close to the beach."

"It's cool," I say weakly. There is no beach in sight.

"Let me run in and get the room stuff figured out. You wait here."

"Okay," I say.

He takes my face in his hands. "Just, one thing though." He seems serious. "I just want to make sure that you're eighteen," he says.

"What?" I ask. I laugh. "You know I'm fifteen."

He nods, like I am an adorable child. "I just need you to tell me that you're eighteen."

"You mean, like how you told me that you're twenty-six?"

"I never told you that I was twenty-six."

"Yes, you did."

David lets go of my face and leans back. He's smiling at me like I'm crazy.

"Um, there is no way that I told you that because it's not true," he says. "You know I'm twenty-nine, right? I wouldn't lie to you about that."

Twenty-nine. I'm not even sure that this is the truth. I mean, I guess he could be twenty-nine. But I know he told me he was twenty-six. I bet I could find where he said it, too, if I had a minute.

"But whatever. I need you to tell me you're eighteen," he says. "Just so that if anyone ever asks, I wouldn't be lying. I would say, you know, she told me she was eighteen."

"I don't actually think that's how it works," I say, shaking my head, annoyed. "But fine. I'm eighteen. Okay?"

"Great," he says, smiling. "You know you're my fucking soul mate?" he asks. He leans in to kiss me again.

"Me too," I say.

When he gets out of the car, I see that my mother has blown up my phone. My voicemail is full—my aunt has called a bunch of times too—and there are fifty-seven texts. I scroll through them quickly, some are just

wtf
pick the fuck up
pick up the phone

And some are longer:

you are the best thing in my life.
Maybe I should have driven you all the

*way to queens but jen said it was fine
and you know what happens*

*when I see my parents
it just puts me into a tailspin
so I have to protect myself too
please call me back sweet girl
I'm sorry for yelling at you before*

about the slushie

*just such a long fucking ride
im done
by hour 9*

lol

just call me back

clal me back

right now you fucking pain in the ass

 your grandparents are having a heart attack

*i am hysterically crying
im gonna have an accident
I am turning the fucking car
around
I will come abck an get you*

Dirty Suburbia

I see David under the halo of a parking lot light, returning. I text her quickly.

*Do not come back
you are acting like a psycho
stop texting me
I am turning my phone off*

*you can yell at me tmw
when I am back at gmas*

I put the phone in my backpack.

***

I wasn't really hungry, but when David said we should get a pizza I thought maybe he'd go out for it so I said yes, I wanted some, but then I realized he was just having it delivered anyway.

We are on the bed, the scratchy bedspread discarded and lying in a heap on the floor. "After the pizza," he says, kissing my bare shoulder, "We are going to go again."

He says this like it is thrilling news. I smile at him and he smiles back. He leans in close to my ear. I can't see it, but I can tell he is grabbing his dick. "I took a pill," he says, lifting his eyebrows and smirking.

I wonder, just for a second, what kind of pill he is talking about and then I suddenly understand and I make a face.

"What?" he asks.

"I mean, how old are you really?" I blurt out.

He looks injured.

"It's just for fun," he says. "It's not cause I *need* it. I wanted it to be special for you. I wanted to give it to you all night long," he says. He leans in again. He nibbles on my ear lobe.

I do my best to smile back. "I gotta go to the bathroom," I say.

When I was a kid, I used to love motels and hotels. I suppose I still do. Just not this one, with its faded green walls and bathroom with only a toilet and a tub. The sink is outside the bathroom, which is weird and also sort of highlights the tub/toilet proximity in a way that makes me want to throw up.

When I come back he is still sitting there, naked. He has a pretty good body, considering he is definitely, like, an old person. You can tell he's old because it's as though his muscles aren't firmly attached to him, like they are kind of just floating there under his skin. And some of the hairs on his body are gray. I realize, suddenly, that I wish I didn't know this.

"Isn't the pizza gonna be here soon?" I say. "Do you want to put some clothes on?"

While he's dressing, I fish my glasses out of my backpack. I quickly touch the towel with the knife to make sure it hasn't come loose. Then I put my glasses on.

"Look at those!" he declares. "You look so fucking cute in those!"

I smile.

He pulls me close to him on the bed. "Those glasses are so hot on you. It's like sexy *Revenge of the Nerds*," he says.

I guess he sees me cringe.

"What?" he asks. "What's the matter?"

***

The night goes on forever. He wants us to take a bath together. All I can think of is being crowded with him in that dirty tub, staring into the gaping mouth of the stained toilet bowl.

I'm not sure how much longer I can go on pretending to enjoy his squeezing and poking and pinching and slapping various parts of my body.

I make a joke, just to myself, that I might have to stab him just to get him to stop humping me.

"So, should I fill the tub?" he asks.

"There is no way I am getting in there," I snap.

"Well, I'm going to take a bath," he says. "And you're welcome to join me if you change your mind." As though I will be just too tempted.

I don't respond and he slumps off to the bathroom.

I get under the sheets and turn my phone on. It's 2:41. As expected, there are numerous new texts from my mother. I don't read them.

I must fall asleep because the next thing I know he is on top of me again.

I use my forearm to push him away.

"What?" he asks.

"I'm sleeping," I say, squeezing my eyes tight, as though that will convince him.

"But I want you so bad," he says. He rubs himself against me.

"I'm sleeping," I say again.

"Put those glasses back on," he says. "I like it when you wear those glasses when I'm fucking you."

"Please," I say, trying to use a sweet voice. "I'm so tired."

"You just lie there," he says. "You don't have to do anything."

"Get the fuck off me," I say, angry now, and I push him with my arm again.

"But I need you," he says, flipping me over and pinning my arms down and breathing into my face. His breath is hot and no longer minty.

"Get off," I say, my voice shaking and squeaky. "You're hurting me."

He's not stopping though, and I actually think, *this is how it happens sometimes,* and I am freaked out by his weird eyes and his skinny-lipped smile. "Get the fuck off me," I say, angry, but not loud. I feel the spit flying from my lips and I feel my face hot and red. "Get off!"

He is holding my wrists so tight, it hurts, but then he lets go with one hand and I can tell he is going to try and cover my mouth. I try to squirm out from under him and I snap my teeth at his hand. "Get off," I scream. "Someone help me!"

He lets me go and sits up on the bed. "What is wrong with you?" he whisper-shouts. "What the fuck?"

I roll off the bed and grab my backpack, fumbling to unzip it and to find the towel.

"You're acting like a crazy bitch," he hisses.

I take out the dish towel and I rip at the masking tape with my teeth.

"What are you doing?" He begins to move around the bed, to come over to my side. "I didn't hurt you," he says, shaking his head. "I never hurt you or made you do anything."

I finally drop the dish towel on the dirty hotel floor and I hold the knife out in front of me in shaking hands.

"What the? What are you doing, Dignity? Baby, what are you doing?" He takes a step back and bumps into the dresser.

"You fucking pedophile," I spit.

"Hey, you told me you were eighteen," he says right away.

He is so fucking stupid that I laugh a little and, even though he totally wasn't joking, he tries to laugh too.

"I want to go home," I say.

He nods. "Okay. Fine. Whatever you want."

***

I hold the knife in my lap all the way back, just in case. He probably shouldn't be driving, and I worry that he will fall asleep at the wheel, so I watch him, carefully, my eyeballs hot and angry behind my nerd glasses, I watch him so hard.

My whole body feels chapped, or like I somehow managed to get a sunburn, inside and out. I am nauseous and so tired, but I watch him.

When we get back to Queens Boulevard, he says something high-pitched and apologetic which I snap off by slamming the car door. He doesn't need to worry so much. I am not going to call the police. I don't ever want to even think about him again.

I am so relieved to be back here, on Queens Boulevard, the Boulevard of Death, at dawn, that I start to cry. It feels so different in the morning, empty save for the pigeons and the few cars that drive by going either too fast or too slow, as though the absence of other traffic has confused them.

As soon as the Corolla is out of sight I dash toward a McDonald's down the street, but when I get there I see only the drive-thru is open. It's too early to go back to my grandparents', so I sit on one of the parking curbs. The air is thick with the salty, greasy smell, and I cry, feeling embarrassed because what I really want more than anything is my stupid mom.

I think about that other McDonald's, back when she made me see my father at the Belvidere Oasis. I didn't ever really know him, but my mother had shown me pictures of him, and, especially when he was young, he was just as handsome as she said he was.

At the Belvidere Oasis, though, he didn't look so good. He was skinny, in a bad way, and he was missing a bunch of teeth, which I saw when we approached the table and he stood up and smiled. On the table in front of him was a Beanie Baby, a stuffed unicorn, which he had clearly just purchased at the rest stop store.

My mother blew out her lips when she saw him. "Well, you look like shit," she said.

"I haven't exactly been staying at the Four Seasons. But you look good, Kir," he said. She lowered her head to look at him with those big brown eyes of hers and pursed her lips to stop herself from smiling. "But who's this beautiful lady?" my father said, nodding at me. "I thought you said you were bringing little Dignity."

"Hi, Dad," I said. He stepped closer to me and hugged me. He smelled like cigarettes and his Carhart shirt was rough against my cheek.

I don't even remember what we talked about, mostly because I was so busy looking at him and imagining him in other situations: carrying an axe, menacing that poor woman, and pushing her into her apartment. I didn't want to think about the rest of what he'd done, but I did come to the conclusion that if he was a stranger and someone pointed him out to me, I wouldn't have a hard time believing that he had recently been incarcerated. He sort of looked the part, unfortunately.

And I also remember just dying in that stupid jacket. I was so hot, like a kitten some up-and-coming serial killer had put in a garbage bag. But I wouldn't take it off, not for anything. When it was finally time to go, I hugged him again and practically sprinted to the doors back to our side of the expressway. I charged outside, gasping at the cold air, and waited for my mother.

When she came out, she looked at me hard but didn't say anything. We were walking toward our car, but then I said, "I don't feel good," and I threw up, so suddenly I didn't even have time to lean forward. It had been chicken nuggets and vanilla shake and ketchup all down the front of my new blue jacket.

"Fuck," my mother had said. She'd stood behind me and used her palms to pull the hair out of my face. "Oh baby," she'd said. "Get it all out."

Later, she'd said it had been a mistake to meet up with my father.

"It's fine," I'd kept insisting. "He wasn't why I got sick."

***

I look at my phone, scrolling through Snapchats, DMs, texts. I find it. Back in March.

Im 26, he had written. *I don't care about the age difference if you dont.*

The person who liked David so much, who thought he was so sexy and funny, who honestly thought he was my soulmate: who was that? Was that me? It feels hard to believe. She seems so far away. And stupid.

On the way to meet my dad at the Belvidere Oasis that one time, my mom had tried to explain herself to me. She told me that when she met my father, she thought he was a "good-loser."

"Like, there are good-losers and loser-losers," she had said. "Good-losers are nice guys who maybe just haven't found themselves yet. Like, Lloyd Dobler."

"I don't know who that is," I said.

"It's from a movie," she told me. "A good-loser's like, not successful, but he's cool. Maybe he's ahead of his time. Maybe he's misunderstood."

"So, you thought my dad was a good-loser?"

"I did. But it turns out he was just a loser-loser." She made a face. "Sorry," she added.

"It's all right," I told her. But, later, right before I had thrown up on my new jacket outside of the Belvidere Oasis, the jacket that my mother had then gingerly unzipped and taken off me and balled up and put in a trash bin with the dumb Beanie Baby unicorn, right before that, I had wondered to myself if maybe she was a loser-loser too. And it made me feel so bad that I had to stop wondering about it immediately.

I was thinking about that again as I sat in the parking lot of the McDonald's on Queens Boulevard, missing my mom. And I was hoping that I wasn't just a loser-loser too. I was hoping that really hard.

ELEPHANT REALTY

Cass was twenty-one when she'd started, and small, so small that at first they didn't want to send her out with clients. But Cass had gotten better at reading people in those months since she'd been cornered in Dr. Cruz's office, and it served her well working for Elephant Realty.

She could tell, for example, when to propose a cigarette break. Back when she'd started in real estate, everyone (or at least everyone on the market for a house) was quitting smoking or had "just quit" and the stress of house-hunting was precisely the excuse they needed to go with the, yes, very-young looking realtor onto the back deck or veranda. Sharing an illicit treat like a cigarette then led to a certain companionableness, trust even, and they'd use her exclusively—perhaps thinking that at the very least she was good for a smoke, and they recommend her to their friends.

Cass made sale after sale. "I guess people don't mind buying houses from children after all," Manda, a senior agent, remarked at the holiday party that very first year.

***

Ten years later and she was still small, still skinny and still smoking, although now she concealed her habit from clients. And she was still making good money. Much more money than she could have ever hoped for had she stayed in academia. If she'd not foregone her senior year of college and plunged into the workforce, she'd probably not have made enough to have been able to buy an expensive condo for herself and a house on the tony side of town for her parents, those sweet losers.

She did miss college. Or, she had at first. She'd loved her classes; she'd loved libraries and lecture halls, the silky pages of anthologies, the almost physical satisfaction of finding the phrasing you needed as you labored over a literary analysis late at night.

Those things felt mercifully distant now, like laughing voices coming through an open window. But sometimes, like when she attended a real estate conference at the local college or when her nephew moved into his freshman dorm, the physical spaces, the smells and sounds, stirred in her a longing for another life so acute it seemed as though she really must get a do-over, that the universe must, at some point, let her return to that dog-eared page, let her try it again, let her revise her life.

***

That Saturday afternoon, Cass arrived early so that she could sit on a wrought iron chair on the back patio and smoke a cigarette. The clients, Kayla and Danny Madden, had been referred by her childhood friend, Joanne Fitzgerald, whose parents still lived in Glen Harbor too, although they lived in the nicer section that Cass now sold in, while Cass had grown up in what her suburban classmates uncritically and inaccurately called "the ghetto."

Joanne had years ago moved to Manhattan, and then to Queens, and, as far as Cass knew, rarely returned to Glen Harbor. There'd been some nastiness, Cass knew, with her family. But whenever Joanne did make a trip back to the suburbs she was sure to call Cass, invite her out for a drink, and, when they were saying goodbye, encourage Cass to "come hang out with me in the city sometime." Cass would smile and agree and thank her friend. Like being handed a flyer on the street, Cass would wait until Joanne was out of sight to toss the offer in the trash.

But Joanne always remembered Cass, as evidenced by this most recent thrown bone: Kayla was a friend of Joanne's from grad school. Joanne had texted Cass to say that she'd given Cass' number to her friend Kayla, "a supercool person." "The husband is kind of a blow hard. A poet," the message continued. "So...yeah."

Cass wondered what Joanne might have told Kayla about Cass. Joanne was not a gossip. Joanne would not say, "Cass has actually been married and divorced twice already." Joanne would not say, "I'm not sure why Cass still lives in Glen Harbor. Masochism?" Joanne would not have told Kayla, "Cass dropped out of college after what seemed to be a nervous breakdown as a result of an affair with her professor or something." No, Joanne would not say anything like that. She would probably say something like, "Cass is a sweetheart. She's really skinny, but don't let that scare you."

When she finished her cigarette, Cass stubbed it out on the slate patio before putting the butt in the empty Altoids box that she used as a portable ashtray. It was then that she heard them, the gravel crunching in the driveway, the slamming doors and family noises. "Human voices wake us," Cass thought, taking another Altoids tin from her hobo bag and popping a mint in her mouth. She used a baby wipe on her hands and then misted herself with a Bath and Body Works after-shower spray before putting all her gear back in the bag to go around to the front where she would meet the Maddens.

The day was hot and bright, but Cass knew relief waited inside the cool, dark house.

***

It was a wonderful house. Over a hundred years old, updated tastefully, with almost an acre of wooded property. And the upstairs "porch" was magical: casement windows showing mature trees on three sides, you felt at once protected and lifted, transported.

Cass rounded the house to see the male-Madden struggling mightily with the "Elephant Realty" sign. It was crooked, the recent rain having caused the post to sink so that the image on the sign—a silhouette of two elephants, trunk-to-trunk—no longer seemed like a friendly meeting of pachyderms, but a display or dominance and aggression, as one elephant pushed another elephant down a slope. Or at least, that's how it seemed to Cass as she watched the man endeavor, and fail, to straighten it.

"Oh, you don't have to do that," Cass called.

He looked up with relief. "I think I'm making it worse," he said. "You must be Cass."

Cass, imagining herself a human lighthouse, cast her smile over the family emerging from the SUV, but her smooth gaze snagged on Kayla, the woman.

She hadn't been quite prepared for people her age, people married with children, who were not simply boring bourgeois. She was usually, if not the cool one, the cooler one, and her clients—even the lesbians—wore Dansko clogs and blousy shirts that did little to hide postnatal tummies. Not that Cass hadn't had her share of Brooklyn clients, self-identified city people (originally from Ohio, of course), tired of lugging strollers and groceries and arthritic dogs up to their third floor walk-ups, who'd not long ago been quarantined in two-bedrooms during the pandemic and who'd gnashed their teeth in bed at night thinking about their smug suburban friends. But those folks believed their very presence, like ice cubes introduced into a glass of water, would increase the appraised coolness of whichever community they selected. And it would; of course it would. But not for very long. Because like ice cubes, they too would start to change, lose their edges. Cass would run into them a year later at Fresh Country Farms and see that they'd been absorbed, their surrender to blousy blouses and Danskos complete.

But this Kayla. She was a different animal.

Stepping from behind the SUV, Kayla revealed herself as enormous. She was the kind of woman who, even if she starved herself, would still be large—tall and broad-shouldered. Other people might say she was "big-boned," but that didn't capture it. It was as though Kayla was a different species, a descendent of Hagrid or the giants in *Game of Thrones*. She towered majestically over Cass and had an inch or two on her husband as well. She wore a yellow maxi dress with spaghetti straps and imagining her naked wasn't something Cass chose to do or resisted; like Alice drinking from the bottle, it was the most natural thing in the world.

Kayla's face was shining and beautiful, her arms adorned with tattoo sleeves, her hair done up in a kind of messy bun not often seen outside the pages of magazines. She held one child in her arms, and the other peeked out from behind her hip. "So great to meet you in person, Cass. I'm Kayla," she nodded in the direction of the children. "And these are our boys."

"Karl and Marx," Danny said.

"Daddy!" the earthbound child squealed, literally stamping a foot.

Cass smiled at the boy, she hoped, indulgently.

"Just kidding," Danny said, winking at Cass. "Their names are Peanut Butter and Jelly."

"Daddy!" the same child mewled.

"I know, I know," the smiling father said. "I meant to say … Peanut Butter and *Grape* Jelly."

The other child, his head resting on Kayla's shoulder, rubbed his eyes and solemnly told Cass, "My name is Quentin. And my brother is Daniel Jr. D.J."

Cass nodded. She never knew the right note to strike with children. She turned to Danny. "Quentin—like Quentin Compson?" she asked.

Danny's beard quivered with delight. "Yes! That's right!"

"He was a pretty tragic figure, wasn't he?"

"How do you know we were thinking of the boy-Quentin?" Danny shot back, so pleased to have caught her in his trap.

"If I'm not mistaken, things didn't work out so well for the girl-Quentin either," Cass said. "Although I haven't read Faulkner in a long time."

"You must have been an English major," Danny said, his teeth big and white in his smile. "And Joanne told me you went to St. Mary's. Me too! What year did you graduate?"

"Oh," Cass said. "Oh." She looked toward the looming house as though imploring it to rescue her, to swallow her up. She felt a red splash, like a sudden sunburn, crawling up her neck, and she was grateful for her long hair. "What year?" Cass had not ever finished her coursework. "I didn't walk. I took time off. And skipped graduation," she said, as though that answered his question. "We probably, you know, just missed each other there," she concluded, nodding.

Danny frowned good-naturedly and nodded back. "But an English major. You must have worked with my mentor, Dr. Cruz?"

Cass shook her head. "No," she said, pretending to search for the key. "I didn't know him."

***

Cass had talked about it a lot right after it happened and then less in the years that followed, but had learned since then to talk about it not at all. Because it hadn't been anything, not really; it hadn't been *rape* and that's really all people wanted to know. Once they found out it wasn't rape they lost interest. When they said, "Oh, so he didn't *do* anything, then, did he," she felt again his hand on her body, his breath on her face. To Cass, it was like saying, *but it was only a small bomb, wasn't it?*

***

Kayla had been talking, but Cass had not been listening. She was looking at Danny's vegan sneakers and thinking about Dr. Cruz, and about what Joanne must have said, and also trying, very hard, not to quiver, and willing the strange blotches not to spread, to migrate from her neck to her face.

It was only the word "Joanne," uttered by Danny, that, like the snap of the hypnotist's finger, broke through.

Cass blinked and agreed, "Yeah, Joanne's the best," feeling as though re-entering the conversation was like trying to jump into a double-Dutch, which was something else that Cass had never been any good at.

Cass bowed her head and moved toward the house. "I wish we saw more of each other," she said. "Joanne's the best," she added, wondering if she had said that already. They followed her up the path and Cass swung open the front door, allowing the real estate to rush in to save her. "It's a truly welcoming entrance," Cass pointed out.

It occurred to Cass that Joanne, like Kayla, was also fat. She wondered if that was what had brought Kayla and Joanne together in the first place: mutual unapologetic fatness. She wondered if it sometimes worked like that. She wondered if Joanne and Kayla each considered the other her "fat friend." She wondered if Kayla would like Cass too, or if Cass was not fat enough.

***

Cass hadn't always been too skinny. What a tragedy to have made it through high school without developing an eating disorder only to succumb to one after her junior year of college! It was such an easy, socially-validated illness to have, though. At her skinniest, people remarked almost daily on how well she looked, even though she was starving and sallow-skinned (a result of the smoking that she'd begun so assiduously that year as well).

Smoking had been everything at first. It was Cass's only consolation. And that was why, all these years later, Cass had remained loyal to the habit, absorbing it into her very self, making it part of her personality. She tended to her addiction the way others tend to their feminine hygiene, their secret love affairs, their IBS: with great discretion and alternating tenderness and disgust.

If she could have hired someone to smoke for her—the way, these days, you could hire someone to walk your dog or pick up your food from McDonald's—she would have, in a heartbeat. Twenty bucks per cigarette break would have been money well spent, as it would have saved Cass all the sneaking around, the small and constant deceptions she felt forced to perpetrate, as well as the scoldings and lectures she inevitably received, the way she fell in certain people's esteem when they discovered she was a smoker. She could almost hear them thinking, "Aha! That's what I couldn't put my finger on about her! She's white trash."

Because at least in the beginning, you would meet interesting people on cigarette breaks. Lately, the only people who still smoked truly were white trash. Or white-trash adjacent.

***

Cass angled herself like a flight attendant and gestured with an open palm. "I think you're really gonna love the kitchen."

Cass finally looked at Kayla again. She smiled and Kayla smiled back. A child darted off and Kayla called, "Quentin, please, stay with us."

"It's all right," Cass assured her. She was about to point out the elegant layout when Danny interrupted, "So, Cass, then. Is that short for Cassandra? Doomed to know the future and not be believed?"

He lifted his eyebrows, as though he'd proposed something spectacular and indecent.

"No," Cass said. "It's not short for anything. I was actually named after Mama Cass." She scuttled toward the kitchen. "The Mamas & the Papas."

"How cool," Kayla said, falling in step beside her. "Although I suppose you're more of a Michelle Phillips. Those cheekbones!"

In the kitchen, Danny waved a hand back and forth between Cass and Kayla. "I see a Halloween costume in your future."

Cass, unsure, or maybe disbelieving, looked at Kayla, who stuck her tongue out at Danny.

"So," Cass cleared her throat and tried again. "They just did these renovations last year."

"You know," Danny said, nodding, "You actually really look like a real estate agent. You're like, the platonic ideal of a realtor. I appreciate that."

Cass smiled and made a small noise, as though she were flattered.

"It's a beautiful kitchen," Kayla said, gazing out the window over the sink into the wooded yard. "I can already tell this house is special. It's almost like falling in love, isn't it? With a house, with an idea. I think I love it, Dan. Do you love it?"

"So far, I love it," her husband returned.

"I can imagine a life in this house," Kayla said. "I can see us being happy here."

***

Cass had talked about it at first, not knowing that talking about it was an even bigger mistake than agreeing to meet with Dr. Cruz at his office in the evening. She'd even talked about it, sitting miserably in a leather wingback chair, to a dean, who informed her that Dr. Cruz was one of their very best teachers, a respected scholar, and by all accounts a tremendous colleague. Cass was informed that this simply didn't square with what they all knew to be true of Dr. Cruz. Could there have been a misunderstanding? Perhaps their signals got crossed. She did know, didn't she, that Dr. Cruz was happily married? His wife was quite beautiful, the dean remarked.

It would seem that these days, people knew better. At least this is what Cass had heard. But back then, which wasn't that long ago, lots of people didn't know better. At least, Cass didn't. And Cass then was not yet a woman, really, which was perhaps why he had chosen to do those things to her in the first place.

***

"Big party last year," Danny was saying. He'd barely glanced around the living room, dining room, and den, so involved was he in his reminiscence. They stood now at the bottom of the stairs, he and Cass waiting for Kayla and the children to catch up. "It's was just astounding how many people he really ... you know, touched. I realize it's a cliché. But still. I mean, there were several teachers, and a journalist, two other poets—one of whom is actually quite good." He cut a glance at his wife, who'd arrived flanked by children, and she smiled, as though to reassure him that he was quite good too. "But what really struck me were all the psychologists and nurses and lawyers who showed up to honor Cruz. This one woman who works in finance gave an amazing toast about how learning to love literature changed her life." Danny took a deep breath and shook his head. His vague smile reminded Cass of the way she and her brothers had always appeared in portrait photographs, the kind taken at Sears or at school: dreamy, angelic. "It was astounding," Danny continued. "It's too bad you didn't get a chance to work with him. I'm astounded you didn't. What year did you say you graduated again?"

"Well," Cass said. "I didn't actually graduate. I wound up leaving after my junior year."

"You transferred?" Danny asked, confused.

"No," Cass said. She felt Kayla watching her intently and she turned and started up the stairs. Over her shoulder, she said, "I actually heard Dr. Cruz was a creep." Once at the top, she looked back at Danny, still ascending. "Did you ever hear that?"

He shook his head, no, his mouth open in disbelief. It occurred to Cass that Danny might be fairly easily astounded.

***

Before the dean, Cass had told her roommate and her roommate's boyfriend, as well as her RA, who'd been the one who'd counseled her to see the dean in the first place. The roommate, unfortunately, also told several people and like an old-fashioned game of telephone, what began as an assault (albeit ambivalently described), was transformed into an affair.

Even now, Cass couldn't bring herself to Google him, fearing her laptop might function as a Ouija board, that in looking him up she might summon him and that he would reach through the ether to send her another (yes, another) email telling her he still thought of her, wondered how she was. That he would feel no compunction about trying to contact her was jarring to her in a way reminiscent of the original insult: it suggested, again, how little her feelings about anything really mattered.

***

Perhaps temporarily chastened, Danny was quiet, holding a child's hand and murmuring assents to his wife's assessments through two bedrooms. They'd come, at last, to the house's best feature, the enclosed upstairs porch, which of course they had already seen in the pictures online, but which was truly a breathtaking room. Cass stood in the doorway to let them enter before her.

Kayla gasped. "How lovely," she said.

The children, unleashed, dashed about, the largeness of the room inspiring joyful movement. Cass, still too-hot and trembling, longed to join them.

Danny whistled approval. "This would be a perfect study. What a room to write in!"

"Who says you're getting it? I might want this room," Kayla said, as she moved, like a dancer, into the center of the space. She closed her eyes and smiled and did a slow, dramatic turn, inhaling deeply, as though she could smell the room's beauty. The children orbited her, mad insects around a lantern. Watching them soothed Cass, and she smiled at the other woman's smile.

"It is lovely," Kayla said, opening her eyes. She walked to a window and leaned against the sill. Cass was surprised at how much she enjoyed witnessing the other woman's delight, and she imagined the two of them, Cass and Kayla, sharing this room, bent over laptops in leather chairs. Kayla caught Cass's eye. "We'll offer asking. We can't go up any further, but Joanne explained the whole 'pocket listing' thing. We definitely need to avoid a bidding war." Cass nodded and Kayla added, "Sorry. I just love it so much. I can't be subtle."

"When Kayla's around," Danny said. "You're gonna acknowledge the elephant in the room." He looked wickedly at Cass and winked. "Maybe you should use her on your sign."

The elephant in the room joke was common enough, although in Cass's experience, it had never been weaponized before. Because she was a prey animal, or a traitor, or both, her initial reaction was to smile weakly at Danny.

And then she forced her face into what she hoped read as neutrality, the face she used when, for example, a boy she knew from her English class muttered "slut" as he passed her at the cereal bar in the dining hall. Or when her roommate had called her to the phone, saying, "It's the professor," and then returned to her Ramen noodles, watching as Cass comforted the man, assuring him that she was fine, something had come up, she'd definitely be back in class next week.

When she finally looked again at Kayla, whose own face was arranging itself, perhaps in an attempt to convey that she was a good sport, Kayla rolled her eyes and said, "He's teasing me." She shrugged. "These past few years—with everything that's going on—I've gained a lot of weight. You wouldn't understand," she waved a limp hand at Cass's body.

Cass wished she hadn't smiled at Danny. She wished she had brought the taser that her second-and-best-ex-husband had bought her for Valentine's Day and which she refused to carry. She wished she'd had it just at that moment. She would have tased Danny until his eyes blew out of their sockets.

***

In his office that evening, Dr. Cruz had broken the rules. For Cass, it was as though they'd been playing scrabble and he'd suddenly introduced dice and declared numeric victory. He had thrown out the rules, changed the game, and then seemed surprised that she was surprised. Taken aback, even. Insulted. How dare she? How dare she.

At first, she'd protested, and he'd murmured, "Of course, I didn't realize. You're a virgin."

"I'm not a virgin," she'd spluttered inanely, embarrassed by what he'd said and then embarrassed by her response.

And then he'd smiled and murmured, "Don't be a tease," and she'd smiled back—why had she smiled back? He leaned toward her again and his lips were soft and his breath smelled of the wine they'd been drinking as they reviewed the grad school application essay that he'd encouraged her to complete even though the deadlines were still months away.

When he released her at last, she'd fled into the darkened hall and, not willing to wait for the elevator, ran into the stairwell, discovering too late that it was already occupied by a clutch of musical theater nerds singing songs from *Godspell*. She flew past them, the noise from her platform mules slapping the steps cascading and echoing, and absurdly, keeping time with the song the theater people were singing so energetically and without shame.

***

"But what was it that you heard?" asked Danny. They were waiting, again, this time in the kitchen, for Kayla to corral the children.

Cass lifted her eyebrows, said, "Hmmm?"

Danny lowered his voice. "About Cruz." He shook his head. "He would never ... He was such an advocate for women. Female authors, female students. He was so ... cool? You know? I can't believe he'd ..."

Cass smiled. A lot of male students thought that Dr. Cruz was very cool. He was not. He was marginally cool. He was cool-ish; cool for a professor. And he was, if not youngish, not oldish either. At least not when Cass knew him. And that had been part of it, of course; Cass, like all the other girls in the class, and some of the boys, had had a crush on Dr. Cruz. So perhaps it hadn't been a misunderstanding after all. Or Dr. Cruz, at least, had understood. It was Cass who had taken years to catch up.

"Dr. Cruz is a predator," Cass said to Danny. "He's disgusting."

"I thought you said you never worked with him," Danny shot back.

"Your mentor," Cass spat, not answering but instead turning to face the sink. She looked at the gleaming pasta arm. She put out a hand and shook it, as though to check its sturdiness. "It's so boring," Cass said, turning back to Danny. "What he did was so boring. It's so boring."

"What the fuck?" Danny asked.

Dirty Suburbia

"I am sold," Kayla said, she and the boys clattering into the kitchen. "And the area is perfect too. You know, Danny's been hired—as a professor—out here, and ..." She stopped short. "Is everything okay?"

"Uh huh," Cass said, turning around to face them.

"So ... we just really wanted to get settled," Kayla tried to continue, a crease of concern appearing between her eyebrows. Cass allowed herself, for a moment, to imagine Kayla and Danny living in the house. She imagined making plans for morning walks, just her and Kayla and the new puppy, the golden doodle the family would get after moving; of course the dog-walking would fall to Kayla, what with Danny being a *professor*, so busy writing his genius *poetry* up in his gorgeous *study*. Cass imagined herself and Kayla and the dog, striding down residential streets at dusk; she imagined them resting on park benches, sharing a smoke.

Cass reached into her bag and pulled out her cigarettes. Kayla and Danny watched as Cass, with trembling hands, put a cigarette in her mouth and lit it. Their faces suggested that they wanted to cover their children's eyes.

"I just remembered," Cass said, inhaling and imagining the smoke circling around in her lungs, polluting her, but also soothing her, killing off all the things that made her hands shake. "This house is off the market. There's another buyer."

"What?" Kayla asked. She wore a confused smile, as though she were waiting for the punchline.

Cass reached around her tiny body and ashed into the sink.

"You won't be living in this house." She took another drag and pointed her cigarette at Danny. "Not everything is for you," she said. She looked back at Kayla. "Someone's already made an offer. Way above asking. Cash."

"What is happening right now?" Danny asked. "Is this about Dr. Cruz? Or about what I said upstairs? That was a joke. She likes me to motivate her—"

Cass interrupted him. "I'm sure you can see yourselves out." She smiled, the fake smile so familiar now, it was starting to feel authentic.

Cass walked past them, right down through the center of the family, and back upstairs, back to that magnificent room on the second floor. She shut the door behind her.

She heard stunned murmuring, parental negotiating. She heard them moving like a many-footed animal, bumbling and blundering toward the front door. She heard the car start and the pleasant crunch of blue gravel.

She took out her Altoids tin and lit a second cigarette and then a third, the room becoming a cloudy, lovely, untended fish tank.

There was no harm done. No one would be bothered by the smell of smoke in the house because it would never belong to anyone else because Cass had decided, in the kitchen, that she would buy it. This room, this view, all of it would be hers. The windows and the trees and the hardwood floors. It was a consolation, after all.

It was so boring, so boring, what had happened in Dr. Cruz's office was so boring. She lay on the floor, her bag a pillow under her head.

She heard footsteps on the stairs and the creak of the door. "I couldn't just leave," Kayla said. "Danny took the kids out for something to eat, but I couldn't leave you like this."

Cass sat up and looked at the other woman framed in the doorway, the blue smoke escaping, curling around her body.

"Want a cigarette?" Cass asked.

"Okay," Kayla said. "I actually used to … I quit," she concluded. She entered and sat beside Cass on the floor. "Are you all right?"

"Yeah," Cass said. "No."

"Danny's a dick," Kayla said. "But he's also … he can also be great."

"He doesn't deserve you," Cass said.

"Maybe." Kayla shrugged and let Cass light her cigarette. "He is actually a really good poet." She inhaled and blew out smoke. "So, did that guy, Dr. Cruz … did he assault you?"

"Yeah," Cass said. "But it wasn't that bad."

"Hmmm," Kayla said. She was quiet for a moment and then said, "I met him at that party Danny was talking about. He was wearing a leather jacket. Indoors. The whole time."

"Yeah," Cass said.

"Do you know if there were others? That he did that to?"

"I don't know," Cass said, although she was lying. She could feel it in her very fingertips; she had not been the only one. "Like I said," she ashed into her Altoids tin. "What he did to me wasn't even that bad."

"Oh, baby," Kayla said. She leaned in and took Cass' skinny body in her arms. Cass's head was pressed under Kayla's chin, into Kayla's damp and sweet-smelling flesh. Cass closed her eyes and, holding the cigarette away from her body, like a sparkler on Independence Day, surrendered herself completely to the embrace.

"It was that bad, baby," Kayla told Cass. "It was that bad."

ANOTHER EDEN

Eden let herself into the Libbys' expanded ranch, only later realizing that, in her enthusiasm for sin, she'd left the outer garage door open.

She'd been distracted, hurrying to put her things among the Libbys' things in the little room that led to the kitchen: her coat to fraternize with their coats, her boring duck boots to learn diversity among their Uggs and Sorels and Skechers.

Snickers came barreling down the hall, flinging himself at Eden's ankles.

"He needs a lot of attention," Mrs. Libby had said when she'd hired Eden to cat-sit. They'd stood in the kitchen, regarding the animal from on high, as Mrs. Libby explained that the cat had been rescued from a fire by Mrs. Libby's ex-husband (even this indirect reference to divorce and re-marriage made Eden blush) and given to Mrs. Libby, ostensibly for their son, Drew, who was away at college.

And Snickers, though plump and energetic, had remained clearly traumatized, leaving cartoon-like claw marks down doors closed against him and refusing to drink water out of a bowl, preferring instead the tall glasses which Mrs. Libby had distributed around the house. He didn't like to eat unwatched; he would only nibble at his kibble if there was not a human in the room. And worst of all: if left alone too long, Snickers would poop and pee on the Libbys' bed.

"You don't want the details," Mrs. Libby'd said. "But I'll tell you this: we needed a whole new mattress."

And so, whenever they went away, Mrs. Libby hired Eden, now seventeen, to come over and keep the cat company. Mrs. Libby had asked Eden to visit with the cat for "an hour or two," but Eden had told her mother that Mrs. Libby had asked her to stay for longer, thus buying herself three or sometimes four hours alone in the comfortable house of a family who had all the devices and all the subscriptions and none of the parental controls.

***

The agitated cat circled and mewled. Eden scooped him up and he rubbed his head against her chin before beginning to meow anew and to twist, demanding to be returned to the floor, wanting to eat and to be petted, apparently, at the same time.

Eden placed Snickers in front of his bowl, and he picked at his kibble, looking up with suspicious eyes after each bite to make sure she was still there. She wished he would hurry up. Like the Libbys themselves,

Eden thought, she was held hostage by this "creeping thing that creeped upon the Earth."

Eden helped herself to a Sprite and, when Snickers finished eating, made her way to the sunken den off the kitchen.

Her body tingled, as though the bubbles from the soda had spread throughout her limbs, making her light, lifting her up to meet this most delicious moment of the day.

Eden's mother believed that Eden spent her time at the Libbys' reading and studying. And Eden always brought a book or two with her; today she had brought *At Home with Grace and Joy: A Guide for Christian Young Ladies* (written by sisters conveniently named Grace and Joy, beautiful blonde women in suspiciously of-the-moment motorcycle jackets), a book which Eden found at once compelling and sickening, like an invitation to sit on her father's lap or to try Pastor Glen's homemade jerky.

But Eden would not be reading *At Home With Grace and Joy* that cold Wisconsin afternoon because Eden would be playing violent video games, looking things up on the Internet, and availing herself of the Libbys' Netflix.

The last time she'd cat-sat (at Christmas the Libbys had gone to Palm Beach for five days), Eden hadn't searched for anything too taboo (she wasn't sure that erasing one's history really worked; Jonah, a guy from church, had once suggested darkly that it did not). Instead, she'd watched makeup tutorials on YouTube and endless, inane TikToks and simultaneously streamed the entire *Stranger Things* series and two *Harry Potter* movies. She'd also logged several hours enjoying the violent video games that she couldn't believe Mrs. Libby permitted her younger son, Luke, who was seven, to play. It occurred to her that the PlayStation might belong to Mrs. Libby's older son, Drew, but then again, she imagined that college students probably had better things to do than play video games.

This time, however, the Libbys were only away for the long weekend, visiting Mr. Libby's sick father in Minneapolis. Eden couldn't help but wonder just how sick Mr. Libby's father was, and whether or not they'd have to go back again, soon, for a funeral. She couldn't count on it, though, so she'd have to really buckle down if she wanted to watch a few seasons of *American Horror Story,* which was a show everyone from church had already seen. But first, she'd play video games.

She set up TikTok on the iPad and turned on the Xbox. The Libbys' house glowed and hummed around her.

***

Snickers, after his initial hysteria, immediately fell asleep in her lap. With the shades drawn against the afternoon sun, the light in the room was a comfortable orange. The sound of gunfire and explosions issued faintly, soothingly, from the television.

Suddenly, alarmed, the cat dug his claws into Eden's thighs and sprang away, darting up the two stairs that led to the kitchen and then disappearing.

Dirty Suburbia

Shaken from her own semi-meditative daze, Eden's first thought was of her mother and, instinctively, she slapped down the iPad, tossed the controller, grabbed the remote, and turned off the television.

But it was not her mother—that thought had been absurd. Her mother was intrusive and obnoxious, but she rarely ventured out, and then only for church and church-related activities.

There was a booming noise from beyond the kitchen.

That was when Eden realized she might have left the garage door open. She remembered being outside, punching in the code as instructed, but had she hit the button to lower the door behind her? She usually did, but perhaps she'd been so eager to get in the warm and happy house that she'd just kept walking, gliding through the unlocked kitchen door and then, of course, leaving that door unlocked in turn.

Her body frozen, her mind raced.

There was no way the Libbys were back. They would have called to let her know. And it wasn't the Libbys, Eden knew, because it didn't sound like a group—there were no voices, no familial conversations, whines and warnings, as they tumbled back into their home.

Maybe it was an animal, seeking out the heat of the garage? But if it wasn't, the door from the garage to the kitchen would open any moment. Should she dash up the steps and lock it? Should she run for the front door? She couldn't. She had wasted too much time already.

At the sound of the door opening, her body moved automatically: she got up and climbed over the back of the couch, which sat at an angle in the corner of the room. The area behind the couch was made more cramped by the presence of several large plastic toys—a castle and a Hot Wheels playset composed of brightly-colored flying buttresses—but Eden was able to shoehorn her backside down, almost noiselessly, just as someone entered the kitchen. Concealed, Eden told herself that even if the intruder came in the room to steal the television, he wouldn't bother to look behind the couch. She'd just have to stay very quiet until he left.

***

Eden had lots of practice being very still and quiet. Especially in those early years, when they first joined the new church and her mother was truly on fire for Jesus, almost every day brought a new round of high-stakes hide-and-seek. Eden and her sister would wedge their small bodies behind the suitcases in the back of the closet or pull the shower curtain closed and sit in the tub. Once, when Eden hid behind the open bedroom door, her mother flew into the room, and Eden, despite her terror, giggled. This further enraged her mother, who growled as she pressed against the door, squeezing her whimpering daughter against the wall.

Eden was not giggling now, although she did have to pee, which was something else that always happened when she hid. She wondered if she would pee her pants;

if they'd find her dead body and know that she'd peed her pants. She burned with preemptive shame.

Was this the punishment for deceit? Like the black ice that collected in the seams of the street, sin had simply waited for her un-vigilance. In her enthusiasm to sin, she'd allowed the devil to distract her, to sneak in behind her.

And if she survived, would her mother ask what, exactly, she'd been doing that had so consumed her attention? Had she been so taken with *Grace and Joy* that she'd not heard the burglar entering until too late?

Eden could smell the musty sweetness of the garage coming in through the open door. The man—she knew it was a man—moved quietly in the kitchen.

Her eyes squeezed shut, her head tucked down, Eden imagined he must feel her presence too. It seemed impossible for him not to know she was there. She thought of whales, deep in the ocean, their silent songs vibrating across thousands of miles. Could the man not feel her pounding heart through the floorboards?

***

She heard various, unidentifiable clatters and thumps. And then the sucking noise of the fridge door, the popping open of a carbonated can, the ding of a cell phone.

Eden opened her eyes and looked up just as Snickers appeared at the top of the couch. He peered down at her and began to wiggle his hind legs, ready to pounce.

Eden held her breath. She'd realized something, seeing Snickers now unflustered and ready to play, like the incriminating cat of an illustrated and abridged Poe story that she recalled reading back in third or fourth grade, back when she still went to regular school.

Eden exhaled thinly and prayed, *Dear God, please let him just leave.* She prayed that the person in the kitchen would go somewhere, anywhere else in the house, so that she could come out from behind the couch and dash to the door, leaving her coat behind, to run, sock-footed on the icy streets, the quarter mile home.

Because she knew it wasn't a burglar who she could now hear urinating in the bathroom off the kitchen—the sound musical and startlingly clear in the silence of the house—whom she could hear in this private moment because he had left the bathroom door open as though this were his home and he was certain of his aloneness. No, it was not a burglar. Because it was, of course, Drew, Mrs. Libby's older son, returned from college.

Snickers plunged down, surprisingly agile, and squeezed himself into an available space between Eden's body and a tub of Legos.

She heard Drew pad down the steps into the den. The couch sighed under his weight.

He turned on the television and a moment later, the room filled with a man's voice, shouting about athletes and injuries.

Oh Lord, Eden prayed. *Dear Lord. I beg your forgiveness and your mercy.*

Snickers, whose loud purring was beginning to seem sort of passive-aggressive, rubbed his head against her calf, against the hand that clasped her knee. How long would Drew stay on the couch? Would he notice her Sprite, her backpack in the kitchen, her boots by the door? And if he did, what conclusions would he draw?

Perhaps he was not one for details. Or perhaps he'd be incurious. Life was full of mysteries. Perhaps, for Drew, the unfamiliar backpack would remain one of them.

He shifted on the couch.

Eden squeezed her eyes shut so hard, she felt as though her face would collapse in on itself. Why had she hidden? Why couldn't she be a normal human being, a person who, when a door from the garage opened unexpectedly, simply looked up and said, "Oh, hi. I'm the cat sitter"?

How long? How long until it was too long, until her mother started calling, or sent her father to find her, or went to the police? What if Drew fell asleep on the couch? What if he had friends come over? Maybe that was what he was texting right now: "Come over, everybody. Let's have a huge, all-night party!"

Eden thought of the pictures lining the walls of the Libby house, of one in particular: a photo of Drew and, Eden assumed, his real father, outside the stadium at a Badgers game. They looked alike in the photo, Drew and his father, brown-haired and handsome, smiling in their red sweatshirts.

It amazed Eden that the guy from the picture was so close, on the other side of a few inches of fabric and wood and foam, and that he had no idea she was right behind him. It was so weird and funny and scary that Eden's body betrayed her, just as it had done when she'd hidden behind the door, and a noise that originated in her upper throat came out through her nose, a noise somewhere between a yelp and a giggle.

She heard Drew leap up; she heard him shout, "What the fuck?" and she knew that in a moment he would peer behind the couch and see her so shamefully crouched.

And so into her knees, her voice small and squeaky, she said, "I am so sorry," and then she opened her eyes and began to stand awkwardly, the plastic castle biting into her thigh as she gripped the back of the couch to pull herself up. "It's just me. I'm the cat sitter. I'm so sorry."

Drew stood, wide-eyed, on the other side of the coffee table.

"What the fuck," he said again.

Eden felt lightheaded. She tried, fruitlessly, to draw her shoulders away from her ears. "I'm so sorry. I'm Eden. I'm your neighbor? I come over to cat sit? I'm so sorry."

Drew blinked with non-comprehension. "Why the fuck are you hiding behind the couch?"

"I got scared when you came in. I'm so sorry. I'm really so ... I'm Eden, I cat—" she began again, a doll with a pull cord.

"Yeah, I know who you are. You're the homeschool girl," Drew said. He pursed his lips, blew out. "But, I mean, what the fuck?" He bent to pick up his phone from the floor where he must have thrown it, and let out a small, incredulous laugh.

Eden stood, hunched and ashamed, behind the couch. She stared at the carpet beneath the coffee table.

"Are you gonna come out from there?" Drew asked, taking a step closer to her. "Do you need help?"

"I'm fine," Eden said. She didn't look at him as she climbed, deliberately and, she hoped, with dignity, over the back of the couch. Snickers, leaping, followed. "I just got scared. I didn't know anyone would be ... I didn't know you'd be coming home."

"Oh my God," Drew said and Eden could see a smile emerging, creeping out into his face. "That's hilarious. I'm the one who's sorry! I didn't mean to scare you."

He flung himself into the over-sized armchair that matched the couch. He was bigger than she'd realized—tall and broad—and his hair was shaggier than in the picture.

"No, I'm so sorry," Eden said, looking at her feet in their socks. Snickers, who had been pacing the couch behind Eden, pawed at her. "I'm so stupid."

"Nah." Drew disagreed, shaking his head. "But you know, you should probably call the police if you think someone's breaking in." He put his hand to his chest. "God, you almost gave me a heart attack. I was just sitting there and you ... I'm glad I didn't do anything embarrassing!" He laughed. "What the fuck," he said again, but gently, almost sweetly, this time. "I guess I shoulda told my mom I was coming home. But it was a last-minute thing. Amber Culver is having a party tonight—do you know her?"

Eden shook her head vaguely. "I should probably go. Now that you're here."

"No, don't go!" Drew bellowed good-naturedly. He rose, as though to prevent her from leaving. "Please, I feel so bad. I freaked you out and now I'm ruining your gig. Hang out. Do you want pizza? I'm starving."

Eden shook her head, unsure of what was happening.

"Please don't go," Drew continued. And then, self-conscious: "Unless you have to, or whatever." Looking at his phone, Drew took the two steps out of the den in one leap. "But I'm personally still recovering. Really. That was fucking nuts. I was just hanging out and you were ... jeez. Do you want a Sprite?"

Drew had opened the fridge and taken out another can before Eden could collect herself enough to answer. Bounding back down the steps, he held the Sprite out to her, an offering.

"Thanks," Eden said, looking at the two cans already on the coffee table. "I don't want to drink up all your pop or anything."

Drew made a face to suggest this was an impossibility. Instead of milk and honey, Eden thought, this was the land of pizza and Sprite. Drew returned to the armchair, looking at his phone while he talked: "No, really, if you leave I'll eat the whole pizza myself and then I'll feel disgusting. So do me a favor and hang out."

Before she could answer, he was talking into the phone, reciting a card number, saying, "You know what? Throw in an order of Pokey sticks." Eden sat, watching him, wishing she could take notes. He was so easy; you'd think it was every day he found a girl hiding in his house. Snickers walked in and out of her lap.

Drew laid the phone on his thigh. "So, wait, Eden, right? Are you still being homeschooled or whatever? Or do you go to college?"

"Yeah," Eden said. The soda was cold and wet in her hand and she put it on the coffee table. "I'm still ... we still do school at home," she said. "But I'd be a senior. If I went to high school."

"Oh, right on," Drew said, nodding.

Eden nodded too. She took a moment to look down at herself, at her grey cardigan and almost-threadbare "I'm a Norelco Millionaire!" tee-shirt that she'd gotten at the church thrift shop—she'd thought it was vintage and ironic—but now it just seemed dingy. Like she was poor. At least she was wearing jeans and not one of the bizarre Holly Hobby skirts her mother was always making and selling on Etsy. And, praise Jesus, she was wearing matching socks. But still. She wasn't sure how she felt about the Norelco tee-shirt.

Drew, for his part, was wearing a hoodie and jeans that fit him perfectly, because he was a normal, non-fundamentalist-evangelical young adult. His socks seemed to match too, but, Eden noted, they appeared filthy and had holes in the toes.

"You like it?" Drew asked. He looked at his phone and then, as though to resist temptation, laid it face down on the coffee table and leaned toward her, putting his elbows on his knees. "Homeschooling? Did you ever go to a real school?"

"Yeah," Eden said. "I went to a secular … a regular school until fourth grade. And then my mom started homeschooling us. It's fine. I didn't like regular school." She shrugged. "So, I guess it's okay."

Drew nodded as though he understood. "That's so weird," he said. "I mean, it's not weird. Sorry. But it is weird, you know? Will you go to college next year? Or is there, like, a home school college?"

Eden smiled, indulgent. "No, no homeschool college. I might take classes online." She didn't say that Pastor Glen had recently introduced her mother to the concept of a "stay-at-home-daughter" or add that her mother already insisted on sitting beside her, just off-camera, absurdly clutching a newly-sharpened pencil, as she listened to Eden's online Spanish teacher, listening so hard for the devil. Eden wondered: what was the pencil for? What would her mother do with a pencil against the devil? For his part, the devil, perhaps also afraid of Eden's mother and her pencil, had not yet appeared during Spanish class—although in late October, when Señora Martinez began to review Halloween words, Eden's mother had slapped the laptop shut, her own face shut up tight and angry. "Give no opportunity to Satan," she'd said to Eden, her eyes accusing but self-satisfied, as though learning the Spanish word for "witch" had been Eden's most secret, sinful desire.

"Cool," Drew said. "Yeah, I did online classes at MATC last year. I wanted to go to Madison, but I didn't get in. MATC was super easy. I got like, a 3.8 and then I was able to transfer, which was amazing. Madison's awesome. Do you ever come down?"

"I was there last weekend," Eden answered, realizing her mistake too late.

"Oh yeah? Did you go to the bars?" Drew's face sort of lit up but then he frowned. "Or, what, did you go for church or something?"

Eden, glumly, nodded. "It was like … a protest?" she said. She looked at the cat in her lap and then peeked up at Drew.

Drew looked back blankly before he furrowed his brow, realization dawning. "A protest? Wait, like, outside the abortion clinic?"

"Yeah," Eden conceded. "Planned Parenthood." She saw herself then, holding up an oaktag poster featuring lurid pictures of dismembered babies and the words, "*DON'T LOOK AWAY.*" There were two dozen of them from church and they huddled together on that brutally cold morning, waiting for the women to come by, to be scolded and, perhaps, saved.

One car had pulled up to the curb and a woman rolled down her passenger-side window. Eden and the others looked over with hungry expectation; plenty of people honked or called out blessings as they drove by. But this woman, frowning and nasty, had sneered, "Today's not even a day they do abortions, you fucking morons."

Pastor Glen had kept his eyes on heaven as the woman peeled off, his lips moving in a silent prayer.

"That is so messed up," Drew said. "Sorry, but, for real."

"Well," Eden asked, shifting, unable to stop herself. "But aren't you against abortion?"

"What? No," Drew said, as though she had suggested they forego pizza for a can of cat food. "I mean, I'm not pro-abortion. But my ex-girlfriend had an abortion." Eden's mouth dropped open, and Drew added, "Before I met her. It wasn't, like, mine."

"But why?" Eden couldn't help but ask. "Why did she have an abortion?"

Drew grimaced. "Because she wanted to go to college?" he said. Recognizing a very specific kind of contempt in his tone, Eden felt it was probably time to leave. She took another sip of her Sprite and was about to pick up Snickers and move him to the floor, when Drew added, with a conciliatory sigh, "I mean, you believe what you believe, right? Like, my roommate is Jewish. I never knew a … a Jewish person before. Really knew them, to be friends with," he said. "So I'm learning a lot about that or whatever. And he's super cool. I tried to get him to come with me, actually, but he was going to a film festival this weekend. I think you'd like him."

Eden, who, to her knowledge, had also never met a Jewish person, wondered why Drew would think that.

"Are you Christian?" Eden asked, her voice a bit squeakier than usual.

"Me?" Drew asked. "Yeah, sure. We never really go to church. But we're Lutheran."

Eden nodded. She felt her face getting red. She knew, of course, that he wasn't really Christian. Asking if he was Christian was as ridiculous as asking if Snickers had a wife. She hoped she hadn't shamed him.

"What?" Drew said.

"I'm sorry. I didn't mean anything."

"What are you talking about?"

"You know, asking if you were Christian."

"But, I am, or whatever."

Eden shook her head. "I just mean ... your family isn't ... Christian like my family is." Eden thought of Mrs. Libby, of her divorce, and she burned with the fear that Drew would know what she was talking about, would be upset and embarrassed if he understood the reference.

"Is anybody as Christian as your family?" Drew tried to joke.

"Good point," Eden said, forcing a smile. "And I'm not like ... I didn't like protesting at the clinic. I just went cause I'm one of the youth leaders and ..." Eden shrugged. "The idea is to educate women, to let them know the realty ..." She trailed off. "But I'm sure your ex-girlfriend really regretted it," she said, generously.

Drew frowned sardonically and looked around the room, as though searching for a hidden camera or a convenient exit. Perhaps, Eden thought, Drew was ready for her to leave too. She didn't like that; she didn't like that he thought she was some weird, pathetic, Christian loser. "Nah," he said at last. "I don't think she did, actually."

Eden nodded, perhaps too eagerly, as though of course she hadn't meant it that way, whatever that way was.

Drew leaned forward to pick up his phone and she couldn't help but notice how his bicep showed up against the fabric of his hoodie as he moved, or the shape of his strong, long fingers. She sipped her Sprite and said, "I guess I'm just really sheltered."

And, still holding the Sprite, Eden angled her face down and then, to her own amazement, peered up coyly in the exact manner prescribed by one of the YouTube tutorials she had studied. And, to her even greater amazement, she watched as a change passed over Drew's face too, the focus falling out of his eyes as he stopped looking at his phone and started looking at her.

***

The last time she'd been spanked had been almost a year ago, but still, even then Eden had been basically an adult woman and, despite her mother and father's apparent belief it was a non-issue, Eden was nevertheless aware that it was gross and maybe possibly basically child abuse. The slaps, hair-pulls, pinches, the extended kneeling: those were each humiliating and terrible in their own way, but the spanking was next-level, perhaps because not only was Eden ashamed, but she felt shame for her mother as well. Although her mother had never herself indicated any ambivalence, Eden almost felt that she had to pretend that the spanking was normal in order to protect her mother's feelings. No, her mother was not ashamed of it; but perhaps, Eden thought, she should be.

This, this eating pizza with Drew and watching *American Horror Story* (Drew had already watched it, but said that he loved it, especially the first season, and insisted he wanted to watch it again), was obviously a spankable offense. Or worse. But what was worse than being seventeen and being spanked, on your bare behind, by your mother? Eden wasn't sure.

***

"I don't know," Eden said. "It might be a bit too intense for me."

This was a lie. Eden had delighted in every gory, perverse moment of *American Horror Story: Murder House*. If anything, she would have preferred to watch the show alone so that she could pay closer attention, horde up every detail to replay in her mind later that weekend, during the endless hours of church.

Instead, she'd been distracted by Drew and by what she imagined would be the reactions he would be expecting from her, an innocent Christian homeschool girl, and then working to generate those reactions, reactions which then, in turn, solicited his gentle pats and reassurances. When the vengeful baby attacked the girl in the basement, Eden had grabbed Drew's hand and he had held it, gently, between his own, only replacing hers on her knee to check his chiming phone.

Drew laughed. "You think that's bad—later seasons are actually worse."

Eden had to go to the bathroom—all those Sprites—but she was afraid to stir, as though Drew were a skittish beast. Or perhaps she was. She wasn't sure who the beast was anymore. All she knew was that she didn't want to leave Drew alone with his phone, with the texts from all the friends that were surely asking where he was, what he was doing, when he was coming over to "pregame." When she'd suggested he was missing out, he'd disagreed cheerfully: "No way! I like hanging here with you. Is that okay?" And Drew had then given Eden his own sly look, first from the corner of his eye and then turning his whole brilliant face toward her, looking for confirmation that it was okay with her. And it was. It definitely was.

Eden giggled and blushed and silently prayed for forgiveness. And then she also prayed, with both sincerity and acute awareness that even an ever-loving Christ would probably find her pathetic: *Dear God. Please let him like me. Please let him fall in love with me. Please.*

***

Obviously, Eden was not allowed to date. To suggest that she might socialize, alone, with a boy, was as unthinkable as suggesting to her parents that Eden and her sister might benefit from some sort of comprehensive sexual education, or that the whole family might take a vacation at the nude beach that summer.

Which did not mean that Eden did not think about love and romance and sex almost constantly; her daydreams—highly-articulated, vivid, often filthy—were how she endured the many long hours at church, and she had more than once caught herself moving her lips during services, as she played out a particularly passionate dialogue. When that happened, she looked around guiltily, but was always comforted to see several other people, ostensibly in prayer, their own lips pulsing, a school of enormous goldfish.

Eden was also not totally inexperienced: she and the other youth leader, Jonah, regularly made out and groped each other in the industrial kitchen before teen group meetings, and although the encounters themselves were, for Eden, strange and passionless, she felt a thrill whenever Jonah would, flushed and agitated, announce during group that he had too much respect for himself (and for women) to date before marriage, that he was strong enough to "wield the axe" against that which tempted him, that he was "on fire for Jesus."

While he talked, Eden would feel a flush spreading across her own cheeks, as she thought about how, really, he was on fire for her.

***

Drew asked if she wanted to come to Amber's party, said that it would probably suck, but still, did she want to go?

Eden shook her head. "I can't," she said. She pulled her cardigan tight, hugging herself. She'd gotten cold, sitting still for so long, only stirring to tuck a long strand of hair behind an ear, take yet another sip of Sprite. "My parents," she said, a vague smile on her lips.

Drew nodded knowingly. "They're real strict?" he asked.

"Yeah," Eden affirmed. "I really …" She shook her head sadly and, she hoped, in a way that was appealing and dramatic. "It's really hard."

Drew, concerned, said, "That sucks."

Eden rolled her eyes. "They'd totally freak out if they knew I was even hanging out with you."

"Oh man," Drew said. He scrunched up his face. "So then, like, how am I gonna see you again?" He smiled, laughed.

Eden smiled back and raised her eyebrows, just a little bit. "I guess I could tell them I'm … you know, cat-sitting," she said.

"Cool," Drew said, nodding. Snickers, as though summoned, emerged from under the coffee table. "I always liked you, Snickers," Drew told the cat.

***

Eden finally went to the bathroom.

Then they drank more Sprites and picked at the remaining Pokey Sticks, and Eden told Drew about her mother's "new birth" when Eden was nine, about how her mother had found Pastor Glen right after an alarming but mercifully short-lived obsession with Beyoncé. Eden told Drew about the Etsy shop and about the hours at church, the winter sun slanting in through high windows in the early afternoons. She told him that yes, she did want to go to college, that she would love to go to Madison, but that it was impossible: they wouldn't like it, wouldn't allow it, couldn't pay for it anyway.

Drew nodded and murmured, frowned at Eden's stories as though he was looking at a difficult, but not impossible, jigsaw puzzle. And he told her his own stories: about his roommate, the Jew, and about how they'd have bonfires on Lake Mendota when the ice was thick enough, and about his work-study job at the library. He talked about his dad; he told Eden that his mother joked that his dad had "never met a woman he didn't want to rescue," and when Eden asked what that meant, Drew explained that Mrs. Libby had grown up hard, that his dad had whisked her away from her terrible family, that he was always wanting to help people, that he had a new, even-more traumatized girlfriend now. Drew sighed and concluded, "I guess it just means he's a romantic."

Eden wondered aloud if it ran in the family and as Drew looked into her eyes, her eyes that she knew were shining, Eden realized that yes, yes it would be just that easy, that all it would take for her to surrender completely to sin was this: a dirty TV show, several Sprites, and a handsome, romantic boy.

***

It wasn't even eight o'clock, but the windows were flatly black, and Eden imagined herself a beloved fish in a glowing tank: well-fed and protected, floating safely in warm water.

But it was time to go.

Drew followed her to the kitchen. "I'll walk you home."

"No, no," Eden said. "Really. It's just down the road."

"Well, it was so cool hanging out with you," Drew said, watching as she collected her backpack, her jacket, her boots. Snickers sat by his bowl, licking a paw and pretending he wasn't watching them. "So, what time are you coming back tomorrow? You know, if it's still okay for me to be here or whatever."

Eden slipped on her second boot and again found herself peering up from under her lashes, looking into his handsome, serious face.

"I would love it if you were here," she said.

"God," Drew said. "You're so beautiful."

Eden, who felt lit up like a lantern, stepped into his arms, her face lifted, her lips parted slightly, her eyes wide open.

He kissed her, his hand coming around her waist and resting on the small of her back, pushing her gently against him.

When she was young, Eden's mother had told her that this kind of kissing resulted in pregnancy and although of course she had since learned better (from her younger sister, humiliatingly), Eden imagined now a watermelon seed passing from Drew's mouth into her own and she swallowed and gasped with pleasure. She pressed herself against him, a sharp awareness of what it meant to truly want, to really be on fire, and she longed for something tangible to mark this moment; she did not want it to end with her departure, but instead wanted a profound and life-altering exchange to take place, for him to leave a piece of himself with her and for her to forever have a claim on him, no matter the cost.

Maybe, she thought, one hand on the back of his neck and the other cupping his cheek, it would be her going to the clinic next. She imagined Drew driving, she saw her mother outside, wielding a lurid sign, "Don't Look Away."

Drew would hold Eden's hand and tell her they didn't have to do this if she didn't want to. But she'd insist that she wanted to go through with the abortion. She'd say, "Um, Drew? I actually want to go to college?"

And although she would be tempted to say, "Fuck you, you fucking morons," to her mother and Jonah and Pastor Glen as they passed, she would not, her head held high with Drew beside her, almost unrecognizable, not the same person, but a more perfect person, another Eden, different from anyone any of them had ever known before.

BACK TO THE BEACH

In 1993, when Paula was a junior in college, she'd met her mother for lunch at a diner off Interstate 80 in Janesville, Wisconsin. Her mother was a bank executive in Arizona. She was tan and wrinkled and very laid back. She'd told Paula, "I didn't feel bad leaving you with your father. I knew he would be an okay dad. But I personally had to get out of there. I was suffocating. He can be really..." She'd waved a hand in the air.

"I know," Paula agreed, although she didn't know. Not really.

Her mother looked down at her plate and then pushed it toward Paula, gesturing. Her mother had barely eaten anything.

Paula took a fry.

"He's been a decent father," Paula said, chewing. "I can't really complain."

"I'm glad," her mother had said. "My father was a real son of a bitch."

***

Because really, what kind of a jerk has three abortions? Paula thought, as she imagined holding yet another clipboard:

Pregnancies: 3

Births: 0

She sat on the sofa with Julian. He had his feet propped on the coffee table and she had her legs across his lap.

"I feel like that cliché. Like I'm who they're talking about when those smug assholes say, 'I'm not against abortion—I just don't think people should use it like birth control.'"

Julian didn't say anything, but he grimaced, to communicate, she imagined, his shared contempt for those smug assholes.

"Although, I don't even have an excuse, really," Paula continued. "I went to college. I understand how things *work*." She put her face in her hands and then peeked out. "I don't know what my problem is."

Julian continued to not say anything. He was still wearing his coat, although he had kicked off his Converse high tops and they sat under the coffee table, sadly collapsing into themselves.

Paula wore her pajamas. She'd called in sick at work to go to the clinic, where she'd been forced to endure a counseling session that was purely performative. The ostensible counselor—who was probably the same age as Paula but who was aged by her ladies' haircut, a true surrender, Paula thought—discussed the procedure, as though Paula wasn't an old pro at this point.

Once back in the apartment, Paula immediately put on what she called "soft clothes" and retreated to the couch to watch daytime talk shows. As usual, *Jerry Springer* had been lazy and sloppy, pitting the poor and otherwise marginalized against each other; *Oprah* terrorized guests with make-unders. Paula wondered how much of a make-under one needed to become completely invisible.

"It's not like you're totally off the hook either," she said to Julian.

"I know," Julian said, looking at her with his blue eyes. "I feel like crap about it too."

"Don't be so dramatic," Paula said. "I don't feel like crap. It's not this grave thing. Ha, ha."

The 5 o'clock news ended. The 5:30 began.

Paula sighed. "I've punctuated the decade with missed periods." She cut a glance at Julian. He grimaced.

"Oofta," he said.

"Do you even get it?"

"Yeah, but it's not a good pun. It doesn't make sense. Maybe you *failed to punctuate*..."

"Fine, it's flawed. I forgot you were an English major." She sighed. "What are we going to eat for dinner?"

"What do you want?"

"I'm not really hungry."

"Helpful. What about Chinese?"

Paula shook her head, no.

"Pizza?"

"Pancakes," Paula said. "Let's make pancakes."

***

Lying in bed that night, Paula did wonder if, either karmically or biologically, she'd used up all her chances. She absolutely did not want a baby, but Paula believed she knew herself well enough to be able to imagine a future-Paula, forty-five and looking very much the same, but thinner, in the way that some women actually get thinner as they age (maybe specifically non-mom women) and with nicer clothes. She would continue to eschew the ladies' haircut. This forty-five-year-old Paula felt desperately, frantically sad that she had not reproduced. She was able to comfort herself with fabulous vacations and a penthouse apartment and maybe several small designer dogs, but she was nevertheless filled with recrimination for twenty-six-year-old Paula, that stupid, selfish, chubby, poorly-dressed slut.

She sat up. Beside her, Julian stopped snoring. In the dim light she could see his eyeballs jumping under closed lids.

She slid from the bed and grabbed a robe that was hanging on the closet door.

In the kitchen, she flicked on the light and opened the window. The apartment was hot. Even in the darkest Wisconsin winter, the apartment was always hot, hot, hot; the thermostat, Paula believed, was just a decoration, a sick attempt to make them feel as if they had some control over their environment.

She saw herself reflected in the kitchen window. She looked lumpy. Things like robes never fit her like they did the people on TV. Was it her body or was it the robe or was it both? *Where exactly did the problem reside?* Paula wondered.

Julian called to her from bed.

She didn't answer. She pressed down the bar on the toaster and when the coils were red, she lit a cigarette. She dumped the too-full ashtray and sat, smoking, at the kitchen table.

"Hey," Julian said. Wearing only shorts, he shuffled into the kitchen, which was separated from the living room by a long counter. He looked at the open window and walked past Paula, returning with the crocheted throw from the couch draped over his shoulders like a shawl. "You okay?"

"I'm great," Paula answered. "Psyched to be missing work again tomorrow."

"You should quit," Julian said, leaning against the counter.

Paula ashed and nodded. "I'm not exaggerating when I say that each day I spend there feels like a small death." Julian opened his mouth to say something, but Paula had been storing this up. She continued: "Like, every day I leave behind a little bit of myself. Dead skin, hairs, biological detritus. And I've been there five years now. Five. So imagine I'm there for another five, ten years. What if there's a guy there—a mysterious guy, a weird guy, he probably works with you downstairs—and let's just say that every night after he sweeps the loading dock, he collects up all the bits of me. He's got a

Dustbuster vacuum and he runs it all over my chair and my desk and the floor around where I sit. He's planning to reassemble it, stick all that sloughed-off skin and hair back together again. A nightmarish-Humpty Dumpty."

"What the fuck are you talking about?" Julian said, sitting at the table. He took Paula's cigarette to light his own.

"A perverse Paula snowman. A Frankenstein monster, if you will."

"Is this about the abortion?"

"What? No." Paula frowned, derailed. "I mean, now that you mention it, I do see the rather obvious ... But this has actually occurred to me before. I've been thinking about this for a while. This predates ..." She frowned even more deeply, too annoyed to continue, and took back her cigarette.

"Uh huh."

"But you get my larger point? That I'm being robbed of myself?"

"You need to quit your job, Paula."

"Yeah."

"You should go to grad school, like you said."

"With what butter and what milk?" she said, referencing a joke, an inside joke, a joke that tapped back into the well of feeling they had between them from the early days of their relationship when, once upon a time, after another misspent Sunday, sobering up and watching TV, Julian had said he had a taste for something sweet, that they should bake a cake. Paula, the pragmatist, had responded, sharply, snappily, "With what butter and what milk?" In those days, back when they could do so, Julian had laughed at her and then she had laughed at herself.

"Why don't you ask your mother for money?" Julian said, not laughing now. "Doesn't she, like, own a bank or something?"

"My mother?" Paula said. "Um, no."

Julian closed and opened his eyes slowly. "I'm going back to bed," he said.

"The last time I saw my mother," Paula said, ignoring his announcement, "Was when I was in college. We met at a diner in Janesville. Janesville!"

"Why Janesville?" Julian asked.

"Because she had a conference in Chicago."

"So why didn't she just come to Madison?"

That this was an obvious question struck Paula with the same force as Julian's earlier observation that her sloughed-skin monster could be read allegorically; both suggested to Paula that she had inadvertently revealed an astounding lack of self-awareness. It was a jolt. She stabbed out her cigarette and grabbed the pack, standing to light another one at the toaster.

She looked at Julian and then past him, at her lumpy reflection in the dark window. "I guess she thought it would be fair for us to meet halfway."

But why hadn't she come to Madison? Why did Paula have to borrow her roommate's truck to drive the long, flat forty-five minutes, listening to a Liz Phair CD that skipped, singing along and pretending she was Liz Phair, pretending she was funny and tough and that she wasn't nervous about seeing her mother, this person who had said, "*Let's meet in Janesville. There's a diner there—the Red Barn or the Red Bird or something. Something Red. We'll have lunch?*" Why hadn't her mother simply come to Madison, where Paula, a college student, had lived and gone to school?

Paula straightened and exhaled smoke. "My mother. She had this long black hair. I think she was fashioning herself after Cher."

"That's kind of hot," Julian said. "But do you think she'd give you money for grad school?"

Paula looked at her sweet Julian. "I don't think I would even know how to ask."

"Huh," said Julian. "Well, I'm going to bed."

This time he rose. He moved close to her, and she held the smoking cigarette away from her face so he could kiss her goodnight.

***

When Julian had moved in the previous spring, he'd brought his extensive DVD collection. While Paula pretended to find his practice of buying all the crappy new releases at Best Buy ridiculous, she was quietly excited to have the opportunity to watch movies too dumb for her to have seen in the theater.

And so after Julian went to bed, Paula ran her finger along the DVD spines, looking for something to watch.

She selected *Back to the Beach,* an eighties comedy starring Annette Funicello and Frankie Avalon.

Within minutes, Paula realized that she found the movie hilarious and profound. She watched silently, frowning, completely absorbed.

The credits were rolling when Julian came back to the living room at dawn.

"You were up this whole time?"

"I watched *Back to the Beach*. It's amazing."

"I know," he said.

"Pee-wee Herman is in it."

"I know. And Fishbone."

"It's a revelation. It's a gift."

"I know." Julian nodded. "Do you want pancakes?"

"'Does Dolly Parton float? Does Michael Jackson have flammable hair?'" Paula framed her face with her outstretched fingers.

Julian smiled.

Paula smiled too and rose and turned off the TV. "Let's watch it together later. I want to watch it again," she said. "With you."

"Okay."

Paula took out the skillet; Julian got the pre-made pancake batter from the fridge.

After breakfast, she showered and then he showered.

They left the dishes in the sink. Paula said, "Don't worry. They'll probably be here when we get back."

***

Paula and Julian worked together at the Law School. They had met at the Holiday Party the year before, when Julian sidled up to where Paula stood, leaning against a wall on one side of a vast atrium. Without speaking, they watched a most-certainly anorexic female student teetering toward a group of her laughing, balding peers.

"I'm Julian," he'd said. "I work downstairs." He said it as though he were asking a question.

Getting drunk on wine in clear plastic cups, Julian told Paula that he'd also gone to UW but that he'd dropped out his sophomore year, that he was a Green Anarchist, that he was an urban hunter-gatherer/dumpster-diver, that he and his roommates stole electricity from the city.

"How do you do that?" Paula asked, intrigued.

"Well, we re-wired stuff in the basement. Honestly, I suppose we're really stealing electricity from the lady downstairs." He added, sheepish, "We also steal her cable."

Paula pursed her lips, no longer impressed.

Julian sipped his wine and shifted on his feet. "So, you're like an administrative assistant?"

Paula nodded. "I work in development."

"Cool."

"Is it, though?"

"Probably better than maintenance."

"At least you guys get to smoke pot in the loading dock," she said.

"True," he answered.

"Want to come smoke a cigarette with me?"

"Nah. I quit six months ago. It's slavery," he said.

She made a face. "I mean, it isn't. But okay. See you around."

She began to walk away.

"Wait," he had called. "I'll come with you."

***

They both smoked in the car on the way to the clinic. It was spring and freezing, so they cracked the windows, poking their cigarettes out to ash. Paula imagined forty-five-year-old Paula mourning Julian's too-early demise from lung cancer. "You probably would've started again anyway," she said out loud.

"What?"

"Smoking. Even if we didn't get together. You probably would have started smoking again."

"No way," he said.

"I think you would have."

"You bullied me into it. You practically forced me to start smoking again."

"That's a lie."

"It is not. You actually said, after we'd been hanging out for like two weeks, you actually said, 'I don't know if I can date you if you don't smoke.'"

"That is such bullshit," Paula said. "Wait, did I really say that?" It certainly sounded like her.

"Yes, you did."

"God, that's terrible," Paula said. "I guess you must have really liked me."

"I was crazy about you," Julian said.

"What about now?"

"Now? I think you're okay."

Paula looked out the window. A bookstore she liked had a huge "Going Out of Business" sign plastered against its front door.

Julian kept his eyes on the damp and quiet street, but he grabbed her knee and shook it. "Wait, are you upset?"

"No," she said. "I'm okay. But I'm sorry I made you start smoking again. I would say we should quit, but I wouldn't mean it. Because I'm not quitting and there is no way I'm smoking outside. So now the only way you can quit is if you break up with me."

They stopped at a red light and he looked at her. "Are you crying?"

"No. It's just the smoke."

"Babe," he said gently. "You know, before we met, I had the hugest crush on you."

"Stop it."

"The only reason I went to that stupid holiday party was because I wanted to talk to you."

"Really? I thought you didn't know who I was."

"I knew exactly who you were. I had *asked around*."

"How come you never told me this before?"

He shrugged. "You'd say I was a stalker."

"Huh. I mean, that is a little stalk-y." She finished her cigarette and flicked it out the window. "This is putting a lot of things in perspective."

Julian laughed and drove. "I was so happy that you talked to me that night."

Paula smiled, remembering. "I liked you too," she said. "I thought you were really cute."

"Back in the days of cherry coke," Julian said.

"Back in the days of cherry coke," Paula agreed.

That was another thing they said, another allusion to the old days, sixteen months previous. Although Paula had at first scorned it as too sweet, Julian was a cherry coke evangelist and Paula eventually relented, developing an appreciation for the sugar and caffeine, especially when coming off a long, beery night. It was just the kick in the pants, she would say, that she needed to survive another eight-hour day in the development office at the Law School.

Like teammates in a solitary sport, like swimmers or runners, Paula and Julian kept improving on their cherry-coke-consumption personal bests. Soon, they were going through six packs, twelve packs, a case every day. They started drinking rum and cherry coke at night, rather than beer, to stay on brand.

Paula had gained five pounds, then ten. Julian's skin broke out and he began spending more time in the bathroom.

Flinching first, Paula had at last declared: "We've got to stop. I love it so much, but I think we might be killing ourselves."

Julian had sighed with relief. "Yeah. I feel like shit."

In retrospect, it was disgusting, of course. But at the time, it had felt perfect.

They pulled into the nearly-empty parking lot. Paula grimaced. "The days of cherry fucking coke."

Julian turned the car off and they sat, listening to the engine click and tinkle. "No protestors," he observed.

"And I thought I'd paid for the full experience," Paula said. She turned to Julian. "Would you really have married me if I wanted to?"

"What, do you want to get married?"

"No."

"Are you having second thoughts?"

"No. I was just wondering."

"Paula," Julian said. He ran his free hand over his tired, handsome face. "Whatever the fuck you want to do is fine with me."

"Julian," Paula said, smiling. "You always spin my shit right into gold."

***

It was just a few months after the holiday party, during the previous cold and damp Wisconsin spring, that Julian had showed up at Paula's apartment, wet and wearing all his coats, carrying his duffel bags of DVDs and socks. He and his anarchist collective had been evicted.

"Want a roommate?" he asked in a falsetto when she'd opened the door.

"What is that voice?"

"It's what Adrian says in *Rocky*. 'Want a roommate?'" he repeated.

"Not if the roommate is gonna talk like that," she said.

He fit himself snugly into her life. He had no stuff other than the DVDs and the socks, and he was agreeable, flexible, sweet. He ate whatever was available and wasn't averse to being sent to the store. He liked drugs, but not energetically enough to actually go out and buy any, which Paula thought was somehow a good sign.

When Paula had told him she was pregnant, he let his lips part as he tilted his head at her.

"What do you want to do?" he had asked.

"Let's get married," Paula had said.

"Okay," Julian had said.

"I'm just kidding," Paula said, patting his hand. "I'm getting an abortion. I already scheduled my stupid counseling session."

"Okay," Julian said. "I mean, so you definitely don't want to just have a kid?"

"With what butter and what milk?

"Good point. So, you're all right?" he had asked.

"Fine," she'd said. "This isn't my first … rodeo?"

Pregnant Paula. It seemed to just keep happening. The first time was literally after her first time; she could be a scary PSA about the very unlucky among us. And then the second time took her by wry surprise too. And then of course there was this third time.

She knew exactly when it had happened. Julian and Paula had ridden down to D.C. in a minivan with Julian's former roommates Carol and Theo to protest the World Bank and the IMF. Paula wasn't sure what the problem was with the World Bank or the IMF, but Julian's friends were funny and nice and generous with drugs.

Once they'd arrived at the protest, the banners and enormous puppets only muddled things further for Paula. When she'd asked Carol, who, despite his name, was a boy, what they were protesting, he had answered, solemnly, "Globalization."

She hadn't had time to ask him to elaborate; a mounted police officer was herding them off the street, back onto the grassy mall.

Paula watched as the woman next to her stopped, stooped, and scooped up a fistful of horseshit in her bare hands and flung it at the cop. In the air, it came apart and shit spattered several in the crowd before landing on the horse's hind leg.

People had laughed, but it had made Paula feel sad. A little for the cop, but mostly for the horse.

Later, when the crowds had dispersed, Paula and Julian took the Metro back to the van, which was parked on a residential side street, to get Paula's coat. When they got there, Paula said, "Let's lie down for a minute." In the back of the van, then, in front of a sad-looking two-family Tudor, they'd had sex under a blanket and it had been so good and so sweet.

But of course, that was when it had happened. Julian had been pulling out, but he didn't that day because, they reasoned, absurdly, that wouldn't be a very cool thing to do in the back of Carol's van.

Dirty Suburbia

***

Paula retrieved the Discman and headphones from her bag and got back up on the table. The one worthwhile thing that the counselor had said was that Paula should bring something to listen to during the procedure. She'd forgotten until, almost out the door, she'd suddenly remembered. She'd turned back to grab it, and her old Liz Phair CD.

She put the headphones on and pressed play. A support person held her hand. Paula shut her eyes.

***

The afternoon was bright and the sun glanced off the cars in the clinic parking lot. Paula blinked and wished she'd brought sunglasses.

Julian put his arm around her. "You feel okay?"

"Fine," she said. "They gave me a valium."

"Nice," Julian said, nodding.

"Let's watch *Back to the Beach* when we get home."

"Sounds good to me."

"Connie Stevens is in it too."

"And Dick Dale."

"Why have you been keeping it from me?"

"Keeping it from you?"

"You've been keeping it all to yourself."

"Ha," Julian said. "Maybe I was afraid you'd leave me for *Back to the Beach*."

"Has that happened to you a lot? Women have left you to get involved with lighthearted comedies?"

"Not unheard of."

"Well," she said. "You're right. I might leave you for *Back to the Beach*."

***

When she woke, it was dark. She was on the couch and the television was off. Julian had tucked the throw blanket around her legs and torso. There was an empty ashtray and a new pack of cigarettes on the coffee table beside her. There was also a note: "Went to Carol's. Be back soon."

She wanted to watch *Back to the Beach* again, but she wanted to watch it with Julian. She felt as though she'd ruined it by falling asleep when they'd gotten home; she'd missed her chance. When Julian went to the head-anarchist's place, he often stayed all night.

But then she heard footsteps on the stairs. The apartment door was opening.

"Julian?" she asked, allowing the hope to show in her voice.

"Hey, babe," he said. He closed the door behind him.

She scooted up on the couch. "What are you doing back?"

"I didn't want to leave you for too long." He dropped his jacket on the floor by the door. He stepped out of his sneakers and sat beside her. "You feel okay?"

She nodded. "I'm glad you came back." She leaned into him. "What's Carol got cooking?" she asked with gentle sarcasm.

"They want to do a direct action when the governor comes to town. Maybe radical breakdancing or something."

"What's the difference between radical and regular breakdancing?"

"Maybe intent?" Julian said. "Context?"

"What about radical Jamaica ska?"

Julian laughed. "Yes! Everybody can do the ska."

"Did you eat?" Paula asked.

"Yeah, but it was gross lentils. Let's order pizza? I've got cash."

"Yum."

"Do you want to watch the movie?"

"I do," she said.

Julian went to the kitchen. "Are we gonna do this?" he asked before ducking into the fridge to get beers. "Should we watch this goddamn movie?"

"Yeah," Paula said. "Let's watch this goddamn movie."

***

"I think the kid is my favorite character," Paula said, shifting on the couch. "I really identify with him."

"I like Annette," Julian said, picking up another slice of pizza, now cold.

"You would."

"Paul," he said, chewing. "Let's watch *Back to the Beach* every day."

"I am one-hundred percent in support of that idea."

"Paula," Julian said a few moments later, balancing his empty plate precariously on the edge of the coffee table and lighting a cigarette. "Do you think someday we'll say, 'back in the days of *Back to the Beach*?' Like in two years we'll look back on the days of *Back to the Beach*?"

Paula smiled, her eyes on the screen. Annette was gathering everyone together for a song. "Like we're gonna be together in two years," Paula said.

Julian didn't say anything and when Paula looked at him, he didn't hide his face. Their eyes met and he said, "oofta," in a small, sad voice, before lifting her legs off his lap and putting them on the coffee table.

"Babe, I was just kidding," Paula said, swiveling on the couch, watching him walk away.

Paula picked up the remote and pushed pause.

Julian took a beer out of the refrigerator and then turned back to her, leaning on the counter.

The lights were off and Julian's face in the glow from the television looked so sweet and sad. Paula could imagine him in the future. Someday, he would meet someone who really appreciated him, who knew what a catch he was. She'd be a serene vegan whose politics aligned perfectly with his. His new girlfriend wouldn't smoke and wouldn't surrender to stupid, self-destructive soft drink competitions. She'd have double-majored in sustainable politics and social justice poetry. She'd have done an internship raising fucking quail or something and she would be totally responsible about birth control.

She probably wouldn't understand the brilliance of *Back to the Beach* though. "I *do* think it's funny," she'd protest, unconvincingly, in her cute voice.

"Julian," Paula tried. "Remember back in the days of *Back to the Beach*? Remember when we lived in Wisconsin and watched an 80s movie about California on the day I got an abortion? Remember we watched it two times in a row?"

Julian looked at her. "I don't remember that yet," he said. He gave her a weak smile. "Sorry, Paul," he said at last. "I'm just done today."

Without another word, he turned and, carrying his beer, padded down the hall.

"We didn't finish the movie," Paula called, twisting further on the couch to watch the bedroom door shut.

Am I supposed to follow him? Paula wondered. And then, *Are we breaking up?*

Paula turned and put the movie back on.

At the film's crisis, Paula was suddenly sweaty and uncomfortable. She kicked angrily at the blanket tangled around her feet until it fell to the floor. The skin on her face was too tight; her hair hurt. She lit a cigarette angrily, as though someone who cared was watching.

She pressed pause again. Up, huffing, she went to the kitchen, to the junk drawer. There had been something nibbling at the corner of her brain, making it impossible for her to enjoy the movie. She fished around and found her old red vinyl address book.

Under M, she had the information listed for "Mother, Mine." She'd once thought that was clever.

***

Pretzel-legged on the couch, Paula held the phone in its cradle in her lap, the address book open on her thigh. She dialed, expecting, really, to hear a robotic voice telling her the number was out of service.

But then someone answered. "Hello?"

As though she was a rubber band pulled to almost-breaking, Paula snapped back into herself. She slammed down the phone.

Her heart pounded with such violence that she wondered if she was having a coronary event. What had she been thinking? Why had she called her? She didn't want to speak to her, not really.

And yet, as the minutes passed and her pulse began to return to just slightly-elevated, in the glow of the Annette's freeze-framed face, Paula found herself dialing again, her eye and finger functioning independently of her mind.

When the woman answered, this time saying, "Hello? Who is this?" Paula waited a moment and then hung up again.

Paula giggled, transported back to junior high, exhilarated by fear and delight. Her fingers itched to dial again.

But then the phone in her hand, in its cradle, rang back.

Paula held the ringing phone down tightly, as though there was a danger it would answer itself.

Paula's heart was pounding anew. Sweat from her forehead slid into her eyebrows and then into her eyes, but she couldn't take her hands off the phone to wipe them away.

Her stomach pitched into her throat as the ringing stopped but then, with the inevitability of a nightmare, began again.

"What is going on?" Julian asked, emerging from the bedroom.

When he saw her face, he said, "What's wrong? Who's calling?"

Paula gulped. "Don't answer it."

"Who is it?"

"I think it's my mother."

"Your mother?"

Paula nodded again. Her eyes felt very wide. The phone continued to ring.

Paula and Julian stared at each other.

"You answer it," Paula said urgently. "Say I'm not here."

"What?"

"Please, Julian," Paula begged.

Julian reached over and took the phone from Paula's lap. "Hello?" he said. He listened and said, "I'm sorry, she's not here."

Holding her breath, Paula could hear a muffled noise: a voice in the receiver pressed to Julian's ear.

"Oh. Right on," he said, in the high-pitched, conciliatory tone he used to talk to real adults. "Look, um, Mrs.

Paula's mom? She's fine. She's right here. I mean, she just stepped out. But she's fine."

Julian nodded grimly and then, looking helplessly at Paula, held the phone out. "Just talk to her," he said. "She thinks I'm your kidnapper or something. She's going to call the police if you don't talk to her."

The phone hung in his hand in the air between them. Paula reached out slowly and then put the phone to her ear.

"Hello?" she squeaked.

"Paula? What's going on?" her mother said. Her mother's voice sounded gravelly and even, Paula thought, bored. "Why do you keep calling me and hanging up?"

"I didn't," Paula began.

"I star-69-ed you."

"I'm sorry," Paula said. "Were you sleeping?"

"Yes."

"I'm so sorry."

There was a pause and Julian, who stood beside the couch in his boxer shorts, looked at Paula with a mixture of concern and impatience. He ran his hand through his messy hair before turning and heading back to the bedroom.

"So ... what's up?" her mother asked, impatient. "Why are you calling?"

Paula heard a click as her mother lit a cigarette. She leaned over and took a cigarette out of her pack too.

Paula held the cigarette away from her face and tried to catch her breath. "I guess I was just thinking about you. Just wondering about you. And then I realized it was late and I hung up."

"Uh huh," her mother said. "Okay. Well. I suppose it's been a long time since we talked."

"Yeah." Paula had a catch in her throat whenever she inhaled. She tried to swallow it. She didn't want her mother to think she was crying. "So, how are you?"

"I had cancer."

"What? Wow. Dad didn't tell me that."

"Yeah, well. He didn't know. I'm okay now. It was breast cancer. I had a lumpectomy and radiation. That was all last year."

"Wow. I'm so sorry. I'm sorry I didn't know or anything."

"Yeah."

"Did your hair fall out?"

"No. I didn't do chemo."

"Oh. That's good."

"Yeah."

"But you're okay now?"

"Yeah." She could imagine her mother shrugging. "So, you know. Anyway. It has been a long time, hasn't it? You're always welcome to come out here for a visit," her mother said. "My complex has a pool."

"Thanks. That would be fun."

There was a pause and then her mother said, "You're good, then?"

"Yeah," Paula said. She rested her cigarette in the ashtray. "So, I had an abortion today or whatever."

"Oh," her mother said.

"I mean, it's okay. I'm not upset. That's not why I'm calling or anything."

"Oh," her mother said again. "Well, I guess that'll teach you to keep your legs together."

Paula paused, then said, weakly, "What?"

"Learn your lesson and all. You know."

Paula laughed and frowned at the same time. "That's a pretty fucked up thing to say."

"Well, I'm just kidding. But I guess it's probably true." Her mother paused. "Otherwise, you wouldn't be in this situation."

"I'm not actually in a situation," Paula said. She wasn't laughing at all anymore. She rose and paced—as far as the cord would allow—with the phone. "That was a fucked up thing to say," she said again.

"Okay, Paula," her mother said. "It was nice to hear from you, but I don't really want to argue. I'm sorry that this happened to you. I wish you had made better decisions. Maybe if I'd been a better mother you wouldn't have—"

"This has nothing to do with you," Paula interrupted. "This isn't about you. That's not why I called you." Paula's face was hot. "I'm not upset about it."

"Sure," her mother said. "You don't sound upset at all."

"What the fuck?" Paula said. "What the fuck is wrong with you?"

"Okay, Paula," her mother said. "Great hearing from you." She hung up.

Paula sat back on the couch and held the phone in her lap. She stayed very still on the outside.

Julian remerged and sat next to Paula. The cigarette smoked itself down in the ashtray.

"What happened? What did she say?"

Paula shook her head. "Nothing," she said. "What the fuck is wrong with her?"

"What did she say?" Julian picked the blanket up off the floor. He moved closer to Paula and tried to put it around both of their shoulders, but she shrugged it away. She shook her head again.

"I just … I thought maybe I was remembering wrong. But I wasn't. That's what she's like. She is exactly like that."

"Like what?"

"Like herself, I guess."

"Huh," he said. "That sucks."

"Yeah," Paula said. She didn't want to smoke, but she lit another cigarette anyway. "Julian," she said, turning to him. "Should we have had a baby?"

He smiled at her, but he shook his head, no. "Paul," he said gently.

"But maybe we should have. Maybe we still should. Like have a million fucking babies and just do that with our lives."

"That sounds amazing," Julian said wryly.

"People do it all the time." Paula was earnest. She was scaring even herself.

"Yeah," Julian said. "They do." He stopped smiling and Paula thought she felt something shifting, something opaque to her, but profound and important. "I'm going to bed," Julian said. "I have work tomorrow. You coming?"

"I'll be in in a minute," she said.

She watched him retreat, again, down the hall.

In the movie, not only do Frank and Annette reconcile, but their son, Bobby, comes around to conformity, eschewing his punk rock style and adopting his father's hair helmet and shiny suit aesthetic. Paula can't decide how she feels about this. She liked the happy ending but felt it was a shame that Bobby's been de-fanged. She wished she could talk to Julian about this, but it's probably too late for that.

Maybe that's what she regretted, after all, that one remark, the one about not staying together long enough to say, "back in the days of *Back to the Beach*." She wished that, for once, she could have just smiled and been nice instead. She wished she could take that part back.

MICKEY MAKES A SALAD

It was a standard happy birthday post:

"For Luke, my ride-or-die, the best guy in the world, and the most awesome dad ever. Happy birthday!"

These superlatives were evidenced by a series of images. The first: Rosemarie and Luke, young and be-backpacked, the Eiffel Tower looming behind them. The second: the two gazing at infant Sophia, their foreheads touching, Rosemarie's skin taut and shining. Finally: a silly one of Luke, red-eyed and wild-looking in a Santa costume, surrounded by howling family members.

Beneath the pictures, the standard comments:
HBD old man!
Happy birthday! Love you guys!
Hope ur celebrating today Lukie!

I looked at the pictures for a long time, my eyes finding the picture with baby Sophia particularly sticky: Rosemarie was aging well, certainly, but there was no recapturing of that youthful muscle tone, that line-free throat.

My own throat constricted and tickled. I was smiling as I typed:

Lol Luke would be husband of the year if he wasn't addicted to porn

I didn't allow myself a moment to reconsider. I just hit, "post."

I stared at the comment, the smile widening and the giggle creeping up, out of my nervous stomach and into my lungs, which began to flutter a bit, and then up into my throat and then finally out, at first a noise in the nose and then a literal "ha, ha," and then I was weeping, crying with laughter, so delighted by my own cruelty.

***

When Rosemarie first told me about Luke's "problem," I think she was probably hoping I would say something like, "Don't worry! Everyone's addicted to porn!" but I didn't. I made a face. I think I said, "Ew." I asked what kind of porn he liked best.

It was her turn to make a face. She said, "His tastes are diverse."

And then he'd disappeared for a month, gone to rehab. Was there anything on earth more pathetic and embarrassing than rehab for porn addiction? She and I made fun of him all the time for it. If he disappeared at a party, Rosemarie would lean forward and squint, extending her index finger and rolling it back, as though using an old-fashioned mouse.

"We don't want things to get in hand, I mean, out of hand, again," I might say.

"That's true," Rosemarie would return. "But he really thinks he can beat it this time."

On Facebook, another comment appeared under my own. A person named Ravi posted a shocked face and then, *nice birthday message!*

I'd stopped laughing, but I still felt elated. My body was light and trembling. I was refreshing the page again when the phone buzzed in my hand, startling me. I'd forgotten it was not a dead object.

A text from Rosemarie:

take that comment down right now

and then:

what is wrong with you?

I laughed again, out loud. And then a voice, from my neighbor's backyard: "I hear you laughing and laughing. What's so funny?"

***

Wolfgang, who'd been panting beside me, whimpered and hid behind my legs. I squinted up from where I'd been sitting, smoking, and staring at my phone. A woman, young and blonde and gorgeous, looked down at me from over the fence.

"Sorry," I said. "I just… I guess… stuff on the Internet?"

"Don't apologize!" she shouted gleefully. "But what is it?" She had an accent I didn't recognize. Later, she told me she was from Germany.

The woman beamed down at me, clearly anticipating something hilarious. She was probably on her tiptoes, but still, she had to be very tall if she could peer over the fence like that. "Hold on," she said, and her head disappeared. I heard her speaking to a child.

I stamped the cigarette out in my "travel ashtray." I stood. I was unsure if I should approach the fence.

"You live here?" she asked, suddenly reappearing, nodding at the house. The July sun blazed behind her, framing her head, making her appear even more angelic.

"I'm housesitting," I said. "For the Sheridans? For the summer. Do you live there?" I pointed at the looming Victorian over her shoulder.

"Yes," she answered. "I am the au pair. My name is Margarete. What is your name?"

"I'm Sue," I answered.

"Want to come over to swim?" She turned and looked down and talked to the child again and then turned back to me. "The pool is lovely. Salted water and heated. Come over and you can tell me what's so funny."

I could see that pool from the bedroom window; I'd often resolved to somehow make friends with the neighbor in order to secure just such an invitation. I hesitated, though. I had just launched a missile at my erstwhile "best friend." Perhaps I should stay home, look at my phone, wait for Rosemarie's next move.

But I thought that a distraction would, in fact, be best. Though Rosemarie would never know it, I could feel smug about the fact that I didn't hang around thinking about her but instead went for a swim with a beautiful person in a lovely warm pool of salted water.

That's the thing about where I live. There are a handful of rentals and then there are also the live-in help—au pairs, nannies, some cleaning people—but most everybody else is super rich, Rosemarie included. Because I am not super rich, but I'm also not an actual nanny or housecleaner, I exist in a sort of weird limbo: the women here can be friends with me, they can trot me out to show that they're not snobs, that they still have friends who don't own homes and who don't have kids. But I'm not like them and I'll never be one of them.

My phone buzzed. Rosemarie had texted:

I really don't know what you're trying to do. I apologized 100 times but you are determined to throw our friendship away. Fine. ur a psycho. goodbye

I texted back:

hahahahahahahahahahahahahahahahaah

Then I looked at the au pair. "That sounds great," I said. "Let me get a bathing suit on."

***

Margarete was twenty-five—older than most au pairs—and this endeared her to me immediately, as I recognized a kindred slacker spirit. She also reminded me of my younger self in some other ways. I'd once been beautiful too. I'd spent my twenties trying to capitalize on my broad similarity to Gwen Stefani (who was, of course, also younger at that time), playing up my fine features with platinum hair and bright red lips, whereas Margarete was more of Jennifer Lawrence: stately, gravelly voiced, and a lot less plastically pretty.

Perhaps unlike this other person, though, when I was in my twenties, I really was a total psycho. Well, maybe not a psycho. But I had a lot of problems. I made a lot of "poor choices." I always thought that the reason I kept finding myself in exhausting, complicated, and sometimes dangerous relationships was because I simply loved people too much. And that might have been partly true. What's definitely true is that when I met Angelo, everything changed. This was something that I'd thought Rosemarie had understood, until it became clear that she hadn't.

"I had an argument with a friend recently," I told Margarete, holding my phone against my heart. "And I posted something nasty about her husband. You overheard me laughing at my own joke."

"Let me see," she said, holding out her hand, her eyes bright and smiling.

I unlocked my phone to show her the post, but sadly, it had been taken down. Apparently, Rosemarie had deactivated her account entirely.

My phone buzzed. Rosemarie's husband, Luke, echoing Rosemarie:

what is wrong with you?

"Her husband is texting me," I told Margarete. "Hold on."

I texted back:

Dirty Suburbia

Oh come on everyone already knew

Three dots appeared on my phone. Then:

My grandmother didn't know. My cousins in Georgia didn't know

I nodded, despite myself. He had a point.

Margarete gestured to an inflatable pink flamingo. "Shall we float around? And then you can tell me all about it."

The child, William, was taking his nap. Margarete explained that he went to preschool until noon and then napped for two hours after lunch. His mother was home at 3 and liked to take him around town to his various activities: soccer, krav maga, library club. "I barely see him," Margarete said. "Which, I think, is just fine with both of us." She set her phone, which functioned as the baby monitor, under an umbrella on the table, and we adjourned to the pool.

"Sounds like an awesome gig," I said, stepping out of my flip-flops, pulling off my cover-up, and approaching the pool. I climbed down the ladder and managed to lower myself onto the float.

"I get bored," Margarete said, shrugging. "I know some other au pairs, but they are working all the time. Most days I have nothing to do. I just sit here. Get sunburns." She laughed. "Or watch TikTok. I like the ones about what people buy on Amazon."

"I like those too," I said. "But they make me want to buy stuff."

"I think maybe that is the point," she said briskly. "You are from here?" she asked.

"No," I said. "I've lived here for a long time, but I'm from Wisconsin."

"Wisconsin," she said thoughtfully. "I haven't been there. Should I go?"

"There are a lot of Germans there," I said. "But no."

***

I first met Rosemarie four years earlier at the Beach Café. We were both waiting for our orders. Rosemarie was wearing a vintage swimsuit, the kind with a torpedo-shaped bra and a modest cut on the bottom. She has a killer body and she looked incredible, like a true pin-up.

"I like your bathing suit," I'd said.

"Thanks," she said. She smiled. "I literally got it for a quarter. I'm Rosemarie." We each took a step closer to the counter at the same time, as though we were there together. "Are you Sue? I think I know you from social media. I think you dog-sit for my friend, Gigi McAdams-Berkowitz?"

"Oh sure," I said. "Merlot's a good dog."

We nodded at each other and waited.

"I just think," Rosemarie began. She looked away from me, away from the counter, and out toward the beach. She sighed. "That name. Merlot. I'm almost grateful. Like, if only more people would so clearly broadcast that they're insufferable? It would save so much time."

She turned back and peered over her cat's eye sunglasses to gauge my reaction.

I barked out a laugh. I had found my friend.

***

"Her husband is really addicted to porn?" Margarete asked.

"Yeah," I said, leaning into the flamingo's neck. "I mean, Luke's all right. But he doesn't deserve her. Really, the porn stuff, it's emblematic. Like, he's just another overpaid, spoiled white guy who doesn't appreciate his awesome wife. She should leave him."

"Do you think this Facebook comment will precipitate that?" Margarete asked. Before I could answer, she rolled off her tube into the water, diving down, and then emerging, bright-eyed, like a voluptuous seal, waiting for my answer.

"No," I admitted. She waited for me to go on, swimming placidly. She hadn't found my story as delightful as she might have expected, but she didn't seem disgusted by me either, so I continued. "I don't think it will change anything. But I want to stick it to them, you know? She'd deny this, but she's always trying to push me into marriage and dating. Meanwhile her own marriage is bullshit. She's actually bi—her last partner was a woman— but she's become like a stakeholder in heteronormative monogamy. It makes me so mad, these inauthentic representations on social media. Those photos are a lie. That 'best husband in the world.' I want to blow it up. I want her and Luke to look foolish. Be humiliated."

"Humiliated," Margarete repeated, dog-paddling around me. Suddenly sheepish, I squirmed on my float and considered diving into the water to hide. From behind me Margarete said, "So, what I think you are saying is, is you don't want to get married?"

I laughed. I felt as though I was talking to a post-modern Dr. Freud.

"Well, you know what they say," I said. "Over fifty percent of marriages end in obesity."

Margarete had completed her circuit and floated in front of me. "That's very funny," she said, not smiling.

***

Angelo and I had never gotten married, which is probably too bad because then maybe people (and by people, I mean Rosemarie) would have taken our relationship more seriously. And maybe his family would have compensated me, or at least given me more than the twenty-year-old Mercedes, which, fine, I suppose they didn't strictly have to, but honestly, I deserved more than that.

Part of the problem was that Rosemarie hadn't ever actually known Angelo. He died the year before I met her at the Beach Café. But he and I were sort of locally famous at that point. So even that day, when Rosemarie introduced herself, she already knew who I was: the local dog and house-sitter whose boyfriend, the gregarious bartender from Lucky Penny's, had dropped dead tragically and unexpectedly, at forty, just out of the blue, as they say.

So, when I met Rosemarie, I didn't have to explain. We'd sat on low chairs on the beach, Sophia lying on her belly in the sand in front of us. Rosemarie had said, "Yeah, I heard about your partner. I'm so sorry. I only knew him to say hello. But he seemed pretty beloved around here." She clicked her tongue. "Soph, stop licking the sand." To me, she murmured, "She's so fucking disgusting."

And that day, I said what had already become my line, the line that I was giving out, because I wanted to head off misunderstandings. I'd said: "Angelo was the love of my life. I'm grateful for the time I had with him. And I'm not interested in being with anyone else ever again."

Most people I told that to would protest. "Oh, honey," they'd say. "Give it some time," or, "My mom felt that way when my dad died, but she wound up meeting the nicest man at yoga."

But Rosemarie didn't say anything like that. She just nodded slowly, her lips pursed and turned down. She said, "I get that."

Over the years, Rosemarie spoke fondly and familiarly of Angelo, as though she'd known him, and she let me tell my well-worn stories over and over again, gasping and laughing at all the right places, even though she already knew the punchlines, the endings: the time we'd gone camping and I'd found a tick in my pubic hair and Angelo had immediately, gleefully launched into song: "A humiliating tick in the crotch!" Or the time my brother Christopher got drunk and started berating me, and Angelo, who rarely got angry, said, "I'm gonna tell you once. You don't talk to Sue like that," and when Chris, looking right past him sneered, "Fuck you, Sue," Angelo took him, literally by the scruff of the neck, and threw him out the door.

Rosemarie laughed and smiled and sometimes even cried with me, allowing me to believe that she'd felt reverence for my relationship with Angelo, that she'd believed me when I said that another romantic relationship would simply be a grim and painful reminder of what I'd lost, like watching someone else's home videos of a less-happy childhood.

"My boyfriend died five years ago," I told Margarete as we floated in the pool. "Losing him was the worst thing that ever happened to me. And believe me: I've had some fucked-up experiences. But Angelo was the love of my life. And it seemed like Rosemarie understood that. Like, she would know better than to fuck with that. But then things started to change. Probably around the time she realized Luke was addicted to porn. Maybe because she was in an unhappy relationship, she wanted me to be in one too or something. She started trying to talk to me about how I should start dating again. She kept suggesting I was depressed or unhappy. I mean, I am unhappy. But that's okay. I don't have to be happy. I was happy once already. I'm not greedy. I don't want a new boyfriend. I want my old boyfriend. Do you know what I mean?"

Margarete blinked and shook her head. "I'm not sure that I do," she said.

"That's fine," I said, closing my own eyes, although I had sort of expected her to.

***

I'd thought that Rosemarie understood that it wasn't just a sepia-toned filter that I'd slapped on my life with Angelo. Angelo wasn't perfect—he drank too much and stayed out too late and was often inconsiderate. I once ran out of gas on the L.I.E. on the way to see a gynecological specialist (everything turned out to be fine, but still, it was a stressful appointment) because he'd been driving my car around on fumes, in part because he didn't have any gas in his own car. And he did shit like that all the time: if a dog had an accident in the house, Angelo would step right over it on his way out the door. Or if I asked him to drop off books at the library, I'd find them two months later in the trunk of his car, under a wet beach towel.

No, he wasn't perfect. But he was pretty fucking close. He was kind and generous and cheerful and he loved me so much. He told me every day, all day long, that he loved me, told me he was the luckiest guy on the planet, couldn't pass me in the kitchen without giving me a squeeze and telling me how sexy I looked in my sweatpants.

I tried to tell Rosemarie that. I said, "I'm still half-expecting him to barge in with some deliberately-flimsy excuse whenever I'm in the shower. Honestly, I don't think I ever took an uninterrupted shower when I lived with him."

She'd smiled, laughing through her nose, just the right combination of sadness and amusement. "You couldn't have locked the door?"

"I always pretended to be mad," I admitted, "but I secretly loved it. I miss it now. Sometimes I'll catch myself almost waiting, listening for the turn of the doorknob."

Maybe I was being passive-aggressive telling her that. It was around the time she'd told me about Luke's porn addiction. By then we were in each other's lives constantly. We walked together most mornings—Rosemarie with her dog and me with whatever dog I was taking care of—and then we texted all day long, like middle schoolers, feeling this urgent need to update each other, to make each other laugh, to garner sympathy and solidarity in the face of the smallest of life's offenses. In the evenings, we'd sometimes grab a drink after dinner or go to yoga (that was more her thing than mine) and then on the weekends, it was like a Rosemarie-Sue marathon. I'd go to Sophia's soccer game and then we'd all have lunch, go to the big box stores, and wind up the afternoon on Rosemarie's porch. It was intense, but not in a weird, sick, way or anything. It was something special and precious. She was my person and I was hers.

Frankly, if Angelo was still alive, I probably wouldn't have been able to spend all that time with her. Luke didn't seem to mind, though. And Rosemarie didn't even seem to notice that Luke didn't mind.

I guess I was thinking that maybe if I told her about the shower thing, she'd make the connection to her own relationship and to the ways that Luke totally took her for granted. He was so busy looking at porn all the time, he didn't even look at the beautiful woman right in front of him. I wasn't trying to rub it in, showing off that instead of being addicted to porn, Angelo was addicted to me. But in retrospect, I realize that maybe she took it that way.

***

For Christmas, she bought me a session with a medium. It was, in all honesty, the best gift anyone had ever given me. I'd mentioned that I'd wanted to consult someone, to try and talk again to Angelo, but I'd admitted I was ashamed that I was willing to spend so much money on something that seemed so pathetic. And I was scared, having watched too many horror movies about people meddling with forces they don't understand. But Rosemarie booked the session and said she'd go with me.

Margarete pulled herself onto a floating chaise, her perfect behind glistening in the sun for a moment before she tossed her body over. I waited until she was settled and said, "Rosemarie got me a semi-private session with that guy, Ric LaVelle? Have you heard of him?"

She shook her head, no. I explained that Ric LaVelle was a reputable, expensive, in-demand medium.

"It was a great gift," I told her. "I had to schedule it six months in advance, but Jesus Christ, I was excited. This sounds crazy, but I really believed I was gonna see Angelo again. I got my roots done two weeks before. I got Botox," I rubbed a finger along my still-smooth forehead. "I wanted to look good, which I'm aware is ridiculous. But still. Angelo would appreciate the effort, you know?" I laughed, remembering.

Margarete nodded. "I believe in ghosts too," she said.

"Okay," I said. "Well."

She waited for me to continue.

"So, at the session. The most amazing thing happened," I said.

She put her hands in the water, like oars, so that her float stayed in front of me. She waited for me to tell her about the most amazing thing.

"We're in a room in Ric LaVelle's ranch house all the way out east, and it's me and Rosemarie and this guy who is there to talk to his dead mom and this other woman who wants to talk to her dead husband. First, Ric channels the mom and the guy's mind is blown. Like the mom is saying she was sorry that treated the guy so bad and the guy tells Ric, tells all of us, that he's gay and his mother was homophobic and he's sobbing, he's so happy that his mother accepts him. It was very moving, although I was also like, okay, good for you, now can we get to my thing?"

I wished in that moment I had my cigarettes; I wished I was allowed to float and smoke, sort of like the old days when I was young and people did stuff like that. I couldn't smoke, but I couldn't look at Margarete either, so I sort of gazed at the house and at the blue sky behind it. I always liked the idea of God and the angels up there, peeking over puffy clouds at us.

"When it's my turn, Ric says right away, 'you're looking for an angel, right?' And I was stunned and I told him, 'yes, I'm here for Angelo, my angel.' Ric says that he'd entered the room when the other guy's mom was still talking because he couldn't wait his turn. And I'm laughing and crying at the same time because that is so perfectly like Angelo."

I started crying again, telling Margarete about it. And I don't know if it's cause she's German or what, but she didn't freak out or try to hug me in the pool or whatever, she just kept floating, waiting for me to go on. At the same time, she seemed like she might actually be a little bored. I caught her glancing over her shoulder at the patio. I think she was probably longing for her phone.

I soldiered on.

"I really believed he was there. I didn't care that Ric went on to get a bunch of shit wrong. Like, he said we were married and I said no we weren't and he said, 'oh, but Angelo feels like you were married,' which is honestly not something Angelo would ever say. And Ric also said, 'I see a cat?' And I was like, 'no we never had a cat.' And so Ric goes, 'a dog?' And I'm like, 'yeah, I'm a dog sitter,' and Ric was like, 'that's it!' But that seems like bullshit to me too because like seventy-five percent of the population has or has had a fucking cat or dog so it's a safe guess, right? But then he goes ... and this is the part, Margarete." I closed my eyes and saw it again: Ric, all Botoxed himself, slick and shiny, his longish hair parted to one side and smooth against his head, like a Ken doll, smiling at me with closed lips. "This is the fucking part." I took a deep breath. "Ric sort of listens and then scolds, 'Oh, now.' Like, playfully. And he says, 'Angelo wants you to know that he still sneaks in to take a look when you're in the shower.'"

Margarete furrowed her brow.

"This was a thing between us," I told her. I wiped at my eyes, which burned with the chlorine and salt. "Like an inside joke. Ric LaVelle was referencing something private. It was something only Angelo would know. And it was exactly the kind of joke he would make." I remembered the literal chill that ran up my spine, and the way I made an animal noise, a noise I'd never heard myself make before. "I fucking lost it," I told Margarete. "It was like, the expression of my grief for once actually matched the grief I felt. Like something had been unlocked."

I remembered bending over and screaming into my knees. Somehow images made their way into my eyes as I keened and rocked and I would see these fragments of them later when I recalled the event: Ric smiling indulgently and the guy with the homophobic mother nodding with understanding. Rosemarie, her eyes wide with alarm. The shredded tissue in my hands, the blue-and-green braided rug. I cried and cried, even after Ric said that Angelo loved me but that he had to go, and that the next lady's husband was waiting, and there was some handler or assistant who escorted me into another room to take some deep breaths.

I didn't calm down, not even on the forty-five-minute drive home. Ric had hit an artery of grief, and I felt as though I wouldn't be able to stop, that everything inside me would just keep coming out until I was dead. Maybe that's how Rosemarie felt too. Maybe that's why she applied a tourniquet.

"Do you want to stay at my house tonight?" she'd asked. "I don't know if you should be alone."

"I'm not alone," I sobbed. "Angelo ... he's going to be there."

We pulled up in front of the Sheridans' house and she turned off the car and flicked on the interior light. She turned to me and put her hand on my arm. "Sue. Calm down. I don't really understand this reaction. Aren't you happy? A little bit? I thought this would make you happy."

I tried to do as I was told, but my breath came in hiccupping gasps.

Rosemarie bit her lip. "Do you need me to take you to a hospital? I'll take you to a hospital. They can give you something. Or do you have something upstairs? A Xanax? Or even a glass of wine?"

I shook my head no; I didn't want that.

"Was this a mistake?" she asked.

Before I could answer, she said, "Fuck. I have to tell you something."

She let go of me and put her forearms on the steering wheel and then she bowed her head, resting it there.

I kept keening, but I was also listening.

"Tonight was supposed to be ... I wanted to ... my intentions ..." she said.

I hiccupped, waiting, the tears subsiding stealthily, like the tide.

Rosemarie spoke in a hurry. "The screener called last week and asked if there was anything Ric *should* know and, like, she emphasized that there was no pressure to tell him anything but that maybe I could let him know if there was something he should look for and I had been kind of joking and I said, 'he was like a Peeping Tom when she was in the shower.' And maybe it really was Angelo, but maybe Ric also, I don't know ..."

We sat in the car, which continued to click and settle, the sudden quiet an echo of my own. I heard myself breathing, I heard myself shift in the leather seat.

"Sue, I am so sorry," Rosemarie said. "I was just hoping ... I just want you to heal and I thought ..."

I got out of the car. I didn't even close the door behind me. I could hear her calling, "Sue, please," and then I heard her getting out of the car and then I heard her behind me, jiggling the front doorknob, trying to let herself in, but I'd locked it. I'd gone right into the big bathroom with Wolfgang—the Sheridans' dog, who was a real scaredy-cat—and we cowered together on the bathmat.

***

I didn't tell Margarete all of that. Still floating on the flamingo, I found that I'd suddenly run out steam, just couldn't even muster the outrage to finish the story. It didn't help that Margarete now appeared overtly uninterested, frowning and sort of gazing off with unfocused eyes. I'd disappointed her: she'd wanted some sort of amusing story, some entertainment, and I'd rambled on about my dead boyfriend.

The baby monitor chirped to life: a little voice singing the ABCs.

Margarete pulled herself out of the pool, glistening and apologetic: "Excuse me. I must get Villiam."

I peeled myself off the flamingo and slid into the warm water. I held my nose and went under, feeling reckless as I thought of how the chlorine and salt would devastate my hair, might even turn it green, but who even cared anymore? Who was I trying to impress?

When I climbed out of the pool, I could hear Margarete talking to William—she hadn't taken her phone with her. She spoke gently in German, and he murmured back, and their sweet, disembodied voices traveled to me at the pool, their voices like wavy lines, like love.

***

I checked my phone. Nothing. I thought about calling Rosemarie but decided against it. I don't know what I would have said if she'd answered anyway. The last time we'd spoken—a week ago, the day after the session, when she'd found me out walking Wolfgang and literally chased me, trying to force me to talk to her—she'd said all sorts of ridiculous and offensive things, like, "get over it, Sue" and "you're wallowing." And then, in the remark that pushed me over the edge: "It's become your identity. Sad Sue. Eternally mourning. It's like you're addicted to it."

I'd stopped walking then, looked at her. Poor trembling Wolfgang hid behind my leg.

I didn't have a comeback, no cutting remark that would put her in her place, so again I fled, Wolfgang and I, running away.

I didn't have a comeback. Not until that day—Luke's birthday. Happy Birthday, Luke, I thought, as Margarete emerged from the house, carrying William, who held a lidded cup. I would have felt bad about Luke being caught in the crossfire, about ruining Luke's birthday, except that I didn't.

"Thanks so much for having me over," I said to Margarete.

She frowned. "Is your story finished?"

"Pretty much. In the end, the medium was a fraud. My friend Rosemarie had given him the information. That's why I'm so mad at her."

"Oh," Margarete said, raising her eyebrows. William dug into the cup with a thumb and forefinger and delicately extracted a Cheerio, which he examined before putting in his mouth. "And so that's why you humiliated her husband on Facebook?"

"Yeah."

She nodded solemnly. "That's good," she said. "What she did was terrible. You'll find another friend." She put William down on his feet and he sank to his bottom, his nibbling uninterrupted. "Come back and swim tomorrow if you feel like it," she said.

"Thanks," I said, collecting my things, feeling a bit defensive. I mean, I was mad at Rosemarie, sure, but Margarete's response was distinctly unsatisfying, like when you bite into a cake that looks like it will be firm but that turns out to be pudding. It hurts the teeth.

Maybe I hadn't told the story right.

***

I thought about it some more, back in the Sheridans' house. I wasn't going to find another friend like Rosemarie any time soon. I'd lost Angelo and now I'd lost Rosemarie too.

I took a shower in the spa-like bathroom. I washed my face and wondered if Angelo was watching. I did feel a presence in the room and I dried my eyes on the towel and looked through the steamed-up glass. But there was only poor, panting Wolfgang.

Out of the shower, Wolfgang followed me as I dripped down the hall. I checked my phone. There was a new text from Rosemarie.

It said:

I am so mad at you ...

but your post was maybe a little funny?

u asshole

I sat on my bed, still in a towel. Wolfgang tried to lick the water from my legs, but I shooed him away. I texted her back:

I'm still mad at you too

Three dots. Then she wrote,

I know. I fucked up. Im really sorry

I didn't respond. She texted again:

Sophia had to do a "graphic novel" project for school and she was uncharacteristically engaged. I knew she was just copying Mickey Mouse—she was using a stencil, but I didn't care—I was just happy she was doing it and not fighting me about homework. She said it was called "Mickey Makes a Salad."

A pause.

Sue. This comic she drew. OMG.

I waited. I realized I was smiling, just a little.

In Sophia's comic, Mickey has machete claws like Wolverine. He literally hunts down each of his friends. He dices them up. Goofy, Minnie, Pluto. He cuts them up and puts the pieces of them—arms, heads, a boot, Minnie's bow—in a big bowl. He makes a salad of his friends!

Sophia was a weird kid, that was for sure.

WTF, Sue. When I saw it, I knew she couldn't turn it in. They'll think she's a psycho. Like, they'll have her arrested or something. So I took it away from her. I was so upset that I took it away and ran out of the room and put it through the shredder. Which, I didn't even realize what I was doing, but it's basically what Mickey did to his friends.

I held my phone, my nose flaring against the smile, the three dots pulsing.

So then I'm like, what's wrong with ME? And I know I just want to protect her, but I felt so guilty. Like, how could I ruin her work and shame her for expressing this latent rage or whatever it is? And maybe this is a masterpiece? So I opened up the shredder and took out all the pieces

I waited. A photo of a gallon Ziploc bag filled with shredded paper, slouching on Rosemarie's kitchen counter, appeared.

I have to put it back together again, Rosemarie wrote.

I waited.

When no new bubbles appeared, I wrote, *I'll bring over some tape.*

ACKNOWLEDGEMENTS

Thank you to Vine Leave Press and, in particular, Melissa Slayton, Alana King, Amie McCracken, and Jessica Bell. Thank you to my Sea Cliff Writer's Collective, Julie Tortorici and Ayme Lilly. Thank you to Melanie Bell, who gave wonderful notes on several of the pieces here, to Sara Kocek at Yellow Bird Editors, and to Leigh Camacho Rourks.

I want to extend my appreciation to all my old Madison friends, in particular, Dave and Angie and Aaron and Mike. Jen and Jason, thank you for sharing my love of *Back to the Beach.* C.O.B., I hope the inclusions of cherry coke and butter and milk made you laugh. I am also grateful to New York friends, including Lisa and Mari and Vanessa, and also and especially Fiona and Frank, from whom I borrowed jokes. I'm not giving them back.

I will be grateful to the staff at the Children's Greenhouse Childcare Center at Nassau Community College for the rest of my life. You have taken such good care of our family, and always with such wisdom and generosity.

Thank you to my sweetie, Jess. None of these characters are based on you, Jess, but if any of them act in a way that is kind, or generous, or funny, or smart, you were probably the inspiration.

Versions of the following stories originally appeared elsewhere:

"Revenge of the Nerds," *Casino Literary Magazine*, 2020.

"Christine," *East by Northeast Literary*, 2021

"Elephant Realty," *Cordella Literary Magazine*, 2020-2021

"Mickey Makes a Salad," *Mudroom Literary*, 2022.

VINE LEAVES PRESS

Enjoyed this book?
Go to *vineleavespress.com* to find more.
Subscribe to our newsletter:

Milton Keynes UK
Ingram Content Group UK Ltd.
UKHW042031230124
436531UK00004B/54